DENVER

HOMICIDE

BY

John C. Dalglish

2017

DENVER HOMICIDE

DENVER HOMICIDE

EASTER SUNDAY

Sunday, April 5

4699 Granby Way
Montbello Neighborhood
Northeast Denver
8:45 p.m.

Tom Hampton pulled his Cadillac CTS into the driveway. Tired, but looking forward to Easter dinner with his wife, he pushed himself out of the car. He had his key with him, but the front door was open, a sign that Carole was expecting him.

Setting his keys on the hall table, he was struck by the sense that something was missing. Not able to pin down what it was, he paused a moment, and his pulse quickening.

"Carole?"

The house responded with none of the sounds he was used to hearing. He went into the kitchen, where he realized what was missing. The smell of Easter dinner. It should be ready to come out of the oven, but there was no sign of a meal being fixed.

Forcing himself to remain calm, he went down the hall.

"Carole!"

Stopping in the study, he stared at her art materials. They seemed untouched since he left this morning.

Fear began to creep in.

"Carole!"

He climbed the stairs two at a time.

"Carole! Are you here?"

At the top of the steps, he turned right and froze. Lying on the bed was his wife, her eyes half open, her bare chest not moving.

His eyes filled with tears as he forced himself to check for a pulse. Nothing.

He struggled to steady his hands as he dialed.

"9-1-1, what is your emergency?"

The calm voice on the other end of the phone was a stark contrast to his own, which quivered as he spoke.

"Yeah, help...I need help. My wife's been shot."

"Is she still alive?"

He avoided looking at the bed. "I don't think so."

"Does she have a pulse?"

"No. At least, I couldn't find one."

The punching of keys in the background filtered through the operator's questions.

"Where was she shot?"

He forced his head to turn toward her. "In our bedroom."

"Okay, but where on her body?"

"Oh...oh, her head."

"What's your name, sir?"

"Tom... Tom Hampton."

"What's your wife's name?"

"Carole."

"I have your address as 4699 Granby Way. Is that correct?"

"Yes."

"Okay, Mr. Hampton, I have help on the way. Where are you in the house?"

"Upstairs in the master bedroom."

"Is there anyone else in the home?"

It hadn't occurred to Tom that he might not be alone. "I don't think so... I'm not sure."

"Can you meet the emergency responders at the front door?"

"Yeah...yeah."

Relieved to have a reason to exit the bedroom, he raced downstairs, the sound of distant sirens filtering in from the night.

Denver County Jail
10500 East Smith Road
Northeast Denver
8:50 p.m.

Just as he pulled out of the jail parking lot, Officer Eric Pope's radio crackled to life.

"Dispatch to Unit 22"

"Go ahead for 22."

"Please respond to a 10-33 at 4699 Granby Way. EMS is on route."

Eric squeezed the mic. "10-4, Unit 22 is responding."

He reached over, hit his lights and siren, and focused for the four short minutes it took him to get there.

Pulling up in front of the address, he put his car in park just as the EMTs showed up. Getting out and moving to the ambulance window, he immediately recognized the responding team. "Hey, Sarah. Hey, Jim."

They nodded back, and Sarah tipped her head toward the front door. "Is the house clear yet?"

"No. Wait here."

A man opened the front door and stepped out onto the driveway. His warm breath produced a cloud of steam in front of his face as his words carried through the chilly air.

"In here!"

Eric pulled his weapon.

"Show me your hands, sir!"

The man lifted one arm over his head, the other holding a phone to his ear. "I'm the one who called 9-1-1."

"Is there anyone else in the house?"

"I don't know. I don't think so."

Eric came up next to the man, taking note of the flight crew uniform. "What's your name?"

"Tom Hampton."

"Okay, Mr. Hampton, I need you to stay here. Understand?"

"Sure."

Eric, stepped past the man and through the front door.

Moving deliberately but with a sense of urgency, he cleared the kitchen, the living room, and a study on the ground floor. Taking the stairs two at a time, he reached the second floor landing and peered toward the master bedroom. A partially naked female lay across the bed.

He went the other direction and cleared the spare room and bathroom before crossing to the master bedroom. The whole process had taken less than three minutes. He checked the body, her cold flesh confirming what he already knew.

He went back downstairs to the front door and waved the EMTs inside. As they headed up the stairs, he keyed his mic.

"Dispatch, this is Unit-22."

"Go ahead, Eric."

"Notify Homicide I need a detective at my location."

"Copy that."

"I need an additional unit for scene control, also."

"10-4."

Eric moved into the garage, where he found Tom Hampton. The man had raised the overhead door and was standing frozen in place, just staring out at the street.

Almost as quickly as they climbed the stairs, he heard Sarah and Jim coming back down. Sarah followed Eric into the garage. "We're not needed here."

Eric nodded, then re-keyed his mic. "Dispatch, we also need a 10-79."

"Copy that. Coroner will be advised to respond."

"22 out."

Eric went over to Tom Hampton, who was still holding his phone to his ear.

"Mr. Hampton?"

"Yes?"

"Could I have your phone?"

Tom seemed confused, as if he didn't know where his phone was. Eric reached up and gently loosened it from the man's hand. After confirming the call had ended, he closed the handset and put the phone in Tom's pocket.

Tom stared at him, unseeing, as if his mind was far away. Eric moved close to the man and forced their gazes to connect. "Mr. Hampton, I need you to listen to me."

Tom blinked a few times then seemed to focus. "How's my Carole?"

"I'm sorry, sir. She didn't make it."

"Are you sure?"

Eric's thoughts went to his own sweetheart, forcing him to struggle with his composure. "I'm sure. Carole is gone."

Tom looked around him. "I think I need to sit down."

Eric guided him over to an old weight bench in the corner, and when Tom was settled, the officer took out a notepad. "Can you try to answer a few questions for me?"

"I…guess."

"How old was your wife?"

"Forty-six."

"How long have you two been married?"

"Seventeen… no… eighteen years this month."

Eric was startled by a voice behind him. "What happened?"

Eric intercepted him. "I'm sorry, who are you?"

"I live a couple doors down."

Eric spread his arms wide and blocked the man's path. "You can't be in here. I'll need you to stay out on the street."

"Is everything okay?"

Eric ignored the question. "Please, back up, sir. What's your name?"

"Ken. Where's Carole?"

Eric steered the man away from the house. "I can't answer any of your questions, Ken. Now, please move back!"

A patrol car pulled up, and Eric waved at the two officers inside. "Can you stretch some yellow tape, and get the area buttoned down?"

"Got it."

Eric waited until the neighbor was behind the flapping yellow crime-scene barrier then returned to Tom.

"Do you know that man, Mr. Hampton?"

Tom's blank stare had returned. "I...I don't think so."

Opting to let the detectives take over the investigation, Eric sat down beside the dazed man, and together they puffed simultaneous clouds of steam into the night air.

After just a few minutes, Eric realized Hampton had started to shiver. Not wanting to use anything from the home, Eric retrieved a blanket from his trunk and wrapped Tom up.

"You okay, Mr. Hampton?"

A slight nod. "How's Carole?"

Concerned about shock, Eric avoided the question.

"Let's worry about you right now. Okay?"

"Okay."

Denver Police Department
District 2 Precinct
Holly Street
9:10 p.m.

The District 2 precinct building was an amalgamation of red brick, gray concrete, and blue glass. Its design was an attempt to fit in with the contemporary feel of the city and had mostly succeeded, except for the overgrown lot behind the structure. From back there, the four-story structure had a distinctly urban warehouse feel.

Homicide occupied the entire third floor, and in keeping with the holiday staffing for Easter, was largely quiet. Detective Katherine Walker, one of the few occupants that evening, was relishing the uncommon silence as she finished up some paperwork.

The senior detective in her late fifties wore her blonde hair short, and if she put on any make-up at all, it was an occasional dash of red lipstick. Her angular face exhibited a wealth of lines earned from her twenty-three years of police work.

As was her custom, she'd volunteered to work the holiday. Without any family of her own, she found satisfaction in letting the younger detectives spend the time with their loved ones. In truth, her offer served another, more personal goal; avoid the emptiness of her apartment.

"Kate?"

Her boss's voice startled her. "Dang it, Frank! Don't sneak up on me like that."

The mostly bald lieutenant laughed, his generous belly, positioned at the level of her face, shaking at her. "But it's so funny!"

"Well, one day, I'm gonna keel over with a heart attack. Then we'll see how funny it is."

"A tough old broad like you! It'll never happen. Besides, you'll be here long after I'm gone."

He was right to think that, of course. After all, he was the only one in Homicide farther down the career path than she was, but she knew something he didn't. She decided now wasn't the time to tell him.

"What is it you want?"

"Dispatch called with a body. You and the kid are up."

She accepted the slip of paper containing the address.

"I'm on it."

He looked around the squad room.

"Where is your partner, anyway?"

"I told him to spend the night with his fiancée, and I'd call him if he was needed."

"Nice. Anyway, the husband found the victim, who's apparently his wife. The coroner's been notified and is responding."

Kate stood, grabbed her department jacket off the back of her chair, and pulled it on. April was a month of transition in central Colorado, with warmth and sunshine one day, a foot of snow the next. Either way, the nights generally hovered around freezing.

She reached the elevator and pushed the button just as the door opened.

"Boo!"

She jumped. "Dang you!"

Standing and grinning at her was Tanner Austin, her latest partner. They'd been together just six months.

"Got ya!"

"Why do the detectives around here get such a kick out of scaring me?

"Simple. It's so easy."

"Well, in your case, I'm your superior officer, and if you keep it up, I'll find some way to make your life miserable."

He ignored the threat. "Headed out to dinner?"

"Nope."

"So where are you going?"

"Me first. What are you doing here?"

"I felt bad leaving you here to work all by your lonesome."

"I'm a big girl, I can handle it. I thought you were spending the evening with Laura."

"She has work tomorrow and went to bed early. I was bored."

"I see. Well, it so happens I'm on my way to a scene."

Tanner's attention immediately shifted.

"Oh? What's up?"

She stepped onto the elevator and pushed the button for the ground floor.

"A man found his wife's body."

"Where?"

"Montbello neighborhood."

"Want me to drive?"

"Sure."

She stood behind her young protégé, called Tanner by most, and studied him.

Just twenty-seven, and green by any measure of detective standards, she'd complained when she'd learned he was her new partner. Frank had listened, nodded, then insisted. He'd assured her that young Mr. Austin had one of the brightest minds in the department, and with no real choice, she'd finally relented.

Clean-shaven, with a mop of brown hair and deep-brown eyes, Tanner reminded her of Dustin Hoffman in *The Graduate*, which made her feel a little like Mrs. Robinson.

She pushed the image from her mind.

They stepped off the elevator and made their way out into the chilly darkness. A light breeze blew from the southwest, hinting at a warmer day ahead, but for the time being, they pulled their jackets tight around them.

The car gave them respite from the cold, and as they turned out of the precinct lot, she glanced at the dash clock—9:15. They would be on-scene in ten minutes.

Home of Tom & Carole Hampton
Montbello Neighborhood
Northeast Denver
9:25 p.m.

As with most scenes they were called to, Tanner had to park the car some distance away. Several patrol cars were on site, their lights oscillating in an odd, rapid-fire dance, reflecting off everyone and everything. It always reminded Tanner of a carnival midway, which he saw as fitting, since most crime scenes had a distinct circus feel.

That's where he and Kate came in—to bring order to the freak show.

They climbed out and walked toward the house. Despite it being a holiday, or maybe because of it, the crowd was already larger than most. Seemed as if the whole neighborhood was standing next to the yellow tape, straining to see beyond and talking under their breath to the person next to them.

Kate found a path around the outside edge, and he followed until they were both under the tape, staring at the house.

Most of the home's facade was taken up by the garage, with a pathway leading around to the side where the front door was located. Inside the garage, an officer was sitting beside a man wrapped in a blanket. When the officer saw Tanner and Kate, he got up and approached them.

"I'm Officer Pope. I was first on scene."

Tanner took out his notebook and let Kate quiz the officer. "What have we got?"

"Victim's name is Carole Hampton. African-American female, forty-six. She was DOA upstairs in the master bedroom."

"Is that the husband?"

Pope looked back at the man in the blanket. "Yeah. His name is Tom Hampton."

"How's he doing?"

"Not good. He keeps asking me how his wife is, even though I've told him."

"Okay. We'll check out the scene, but in the meantime, let's get EMTs out here to look at him."

"Yes, ma'am."

Kate headed off in the direction of the house, Tanner following behind. He had become accustomed to trailing her, and, in fact, he was more than happy to watch, listen, and learn.

His prior experience as a detective entailed two years in the property crimes division. He'd never seen a body in his whole time there, so when he'd first learned about his promotion to Homicide, he'd been pleasantly surprised. However, when he found out who his partner was going to be, his reaction had turned to one of nervous apprehension.

18

Kate Walker was legendary in the Denver Police community. Known as the Steel Maiden for her icy interrogation demeanor—and her unmarried status—she had faced off against some of the worst Denver's underbelly had to offer.

Rumor had it she'd once made a serial murderer cry for his momma.

Still, as he watched her go up the stairs ahead of him, he now recognized how fortunate he'd been to be partnered with her. It turned out the only people who needed to be afraid of Detective Walker were the ones she was hunting.

They reached the landing and stopped, staring at the crime scene from afar. It was a ritual with her, taking in the overall picture before entering it. She wanted to lock in a mental photograph, as if she was a stranger on the outside who was looking in. She hadn't explained why, and he'd seen no reason to ask.

Watch, listen, and learn.

The lieutenant had given him that advice when he'd been assigned, and Tanner made a habit of repeating it to himself regularly.

Before they moved forward into the room, she turned and looked at him.

"Read the scene, Tanner. Find the story."

He nodded at her instruction, now part of his psyche since becoming her partner.

Carole Hampton was sprawled on her back across the bed, her eyes mostly closed, and her hands by her side. Her hair hanging loose when she died, and got pinned under her head when she fell. The result was a stretching of the skin on her forehead, where two small holes were obvious just below the hairline.

She was naked from the waist up, a black skirt covering her bottom half. Her feet were bare. Kate punched a button on her tape recorder.

"Bed is made, only light on is a bedside lamp, victim's blouse is on the floor to the right of the bed..." She turned and looked at the rest of the room. "Closet doors open, bench is pulled away from make-up table, curtains are drawn, no furniture is turned over, no drawers are open."

She leaned over and looked at a pillow next to the woman's head. "Blood on pillowcase and holes in the pillow indicate it may have been over victim's face at time of shooting."

Tanner stepped over by the make-up bench, which sat in the middle of the room, and kneeled down to look closer. "What do you make of this?"

She clicked off her recorder and kneeled down beside him. In the plush white carpet was a depression, clearly from something heavy.

"I'm not sure. A box or bag of some kind."

The depression was six inches wide but nearly twenty-four inches long, and whatever caused it had been resting at the base of the bench. Tanner stood and scanned the room.

"I don't see anything that fits it, do you?"

Kate shook her head. "Let's make sure we get a good photo."

As if on cue, the forensic team arrived. Kate let them know what her priorities were.

"Get good shots of this bench and the area on the floor around it. Also, after photos are done, let's take the bench back to the lab to be processed."

"Yes, ma'am."

"Has anybody seen the M.E?"

A series of shoulder shrugs were the response.

She looked at her partner. "Let's take a look around the rest of the house."

Back downstairs, they put on a new set of gloves and made their way through the kitchen, where Tanner checked the back door.

"Locked."

In the living room, a sliding glass door led out onto a back deck. Kate tried it.

"Locked. Check the windows."

He did, confirming everything was buttoned up tight.

The only exterior access to the study was a single window, which was also locked.

An easel and some drawing items were at one end of the room, and a large, oak desk took up most of the opposite end.

Kate pointed at the organized desktop. "You could learn something from them about tidiness, Tanner."

"That level of neatness is the sign of a sick mind."

"Is that so?"

He grinned at her. "Except, of course, in your case."

She raised an eyebrow. "Are you sure?"

He couldn't tell if she was joking or not. He opted to change the subject.

"There isn't any sign of forced entry."

"No."

They moved back into the garage, where a white Mercedes coupe was parked. A black Cadillac CTS was in the driveway. Kate gestured at the two vehicles.

"Let's make sure we get the story on both of these. We need to have them processed, as well."

Tanner nodded just as the coroner's van pulled up. Unexpectedly, the Chief Medical Examiner herself got out.

Kate's surprise was clear.

"Dana? What are you doing out here?"

Dana McCloud had been Denver's medical examiner for almost six years.

"Can't let you have all the fun, Kate."

Her long brown hair, green eyes, and round face served to hide her age. Though she was forty-three, the coroner easily passed for ten years younger.

Kate smiled. "Fair enough, but I thought you'd be home with the little ones."

"My family all left town to go back home this morning, so I let the crew have the evening off. What have you got for me?"

"Right this way and I'll fill you in. Tanner, can you check on Mr. Hampton?"

"Sure. Hi, Dr. McCloud."

Dana grabbed her work case from the side door. "Hey, Tanner."

As the two women headed back into the house, Tanner walked to where the ambulance had parked near the end of the driveway. He found Tom Hampton belted into a stretcher. Sarah was putting an IV line into his arm.

"Hey, Sarah. Long time, no see."

"Yeah, we were just down the road when they sent us back."

"How's he doing?"

"Not his best day. We've decided to transport him to the hospital for observation."

"Okay. We'll catch up with him there."

Back upstairs in the bedroom, Tanner found Dana examining the body while flashes from the photographer's camera randomly illuminated the entire room.

Kate kept her eyes on Dana, even though she was talking to Tanner. "How is he?"

"They're taking him to the hospital for observation."

"Okay."

They watched a few minutes longer as Dana shined a flashlight over the entire exposed portion of Mrs. Hampton's body. Tanner liked the coroner and marveled at what a cheery person she was, despite the depressing nature of her work.

He had attended more than one autopsy, where she would slice open a body, make some notations, then smile and banter with her techs, as if they were playing pool at the local pub. Nevertheless, it wasn't a lack of compassion that caused her to conduct herself that way, but because she found what she did to be both challenging and rewarding.

She snapped the flashlight off.

"Tanner, give me hand?"

"Sure."

He took the legs while Dana grabbed the shoulders, and together they rolled Carole Hampton onto her side. Blood had congealed beneath the woman's head, but other than the two gunshots, there were no other obvious injuries. The lack of exit wounds on the back of the head indicated the bullets were still inside the victim.

They rolled the body to its original position.

Dana stood and removed her gloves. "Did you find any shell casings?"

Tanner shook his head. "Either they were picked up, or a revolver was used."

"Well, the pillow may have slowed the slugs enough to prevent them from being through-and-through shots, but it's also likely they were small caliber, too."

"What about TOD?"

"Best guess, two to four hours ago."

Kate looked at her watch. "Six to eight o'clock."

Dana nodded. "Sounds about right. Let me know when you're done, and I'll transport her."

Kate looked at Tanner, and when he shrugged, she nodded to the M.E. "She's all yours, Dana."

"Okay. I'll let you know when the autopsy is done."

Kate headed for the door.

Tanner fell in step beside her. "Now what?"

"Let's get the neighborhood canvas started, then we can catch up with Mr. Hampton."

"Sounds good."

Back downstairs, they spotted Officer Pope still on the scene and helping to keep the crowd at bay.

Kate waved at him. "Officer?"

Pope joined them in the garage. "Ma'am?"

"Did Mr. Hampton give you a statement?"

"Just that he and his wife had been married eighteen years, and they were supposed to have Easter dinner together this evening."

She looked at Tanner. "I don't remember any sign of a dinner being cooked, do you?"

"No, but maybe they were going out."

"Maybe. Pope, do you know who these cars belong to?"

"Yeah. The white one is Mrs. Hampton's, and the Caddy belongs to Tom Hampton."

"Okay. Can I get you to organize a neighborhood canvas?"

"Of course."

"Thank you. Make sure the reports go directly to my desk."

"Yes, ma'am."

Kate wandered over to the Mercedes and stared through the window. Tanner did the same on the passenger side. The interior matched the exterior, with white leather and white carpet, and it was obvious there had not been a struggle inside the car.

They moved over to the Cadillac and checked it. It was equally clean.

Kate stood up and looked across the top of the car.

"So, Tanner, did you find out where they took Mr. Hampton?"

"UCH."

"Perfect. We'll make sure the cars are handled properly, then off we go."

"Copy that."

University of Colorado Hospital
Aurora, Colorado
East of Denver
11:00 p.m.

The University of Colorado Hospital was located east of downtown Denver, not far from the Montbello neighborhood. The large complex of multiple, ten-story structures, all with curved fronts, served as a premier teaching hospital. Because of this, it bustled with activity at all hours. Easter had not changed that.

Parking west of the hospital, in front of the emergency wing, they moved out of the chilly air and into the brightly lit interior of a major medical center. Stopping at the check-in desk, Kate held up her badge.

"I'm Detective Walker. We're here to see a Tom Hampton."

The nurse, a young woman who didn't appear to be interested in the badge or in them, turned to look at the admissions board on the wall.

"He's in bay 6."

Kate stared at the girl, waiting.

The nurse had returned to being uninterested, and when she didn't look up, Kate leaned over the counter.

"I wonder where bay 6 is. Do you know, Tanner?"

"I'm not sure. It looks like there are a lot of bays in here, and I don't see any numbers."

The nurse lifted her head to find she was nose to nose with Kate. Startled, she rolled her chair back away from the detective.

"That way. Sixth curtain on your right."

Kate sighed then shrugged. "See, I would have guessed the other direction."

Tanner counted the curtained bays as they walked, and it turned out Tom Hampton's was not drawn shut. They found him alone and with his eyes closed, but his lids fluttered open when they entered.

Kate stopped by the side of the bed.

"Mr. Hampton, I'm Detective Walker. This is my partner, Detective Austin. Do you feel up to answering a few questions?"

Tanner positioned himself at the foot of the bed and pulled out his notepad.

Hampton nodded slowly just as a man in a white coat came into the room. Wearing a stethoscope around his neck, he appeared to be a med-student rather than a doctor.

"Can I help you?"

Tanner found his badge first.

"Detective Austin. My partner and I are investigating the death of Mr. Hampton's wife."

"I don't know how much help he'll be. We just gave him a sedative that'll make him pretty groggy for the next few hours."

"We only need a few minutes."

Tom held up his hand. "I'm okay, Doc."

"Very well. I'll be back shortly."

Once the doctor was gone, Kate turned back to Tom.

"Sir, I'm very sorry for your loss."

"Thank you, Detective."

Tanner was encouraged to see that Hampton had at least reached the point of recognizing his wife was dead. Kate grabbed a chair and sat.

"Can you tell us what happened?"

Tom shifted uncomfortably.

"Well, not much to tell, really. I got in from Las Vegas and headed home."

"Las Vegas?"

"Yeah. I'm a pilot for Southwest. I got in to DIA around 6:45 or so."

"I see."

She looked at Tanner, and he nodded; Denver International would be their next stop.

Turning back to Tom, whose eyes were beginning to droop noticeably, she raised her voice. "What time did you get home?"

"About 8:15. Carole was supposed to have an Easter dinner ready, but I knew something was wrong as soon as I came through the door."

"What told you that?"

"The smell, or rather, the lack of one. Carole usually makes a leg of lamb, and the whole house smells wonderful. There was no aroma of food when I arrived home."

Kate smiled softly. "I love roasted lamb. What did you do then?"

"I called out for her but got no answer. When I went up to the bedroom... Well, that's when I found her."

Tom's eyes were nearly closed.

"Was the front door locked?"

With obvious effort, Tom tried to remember. "No, I don't think so, but that wouldn't be...unusual."

Hampton's eyes closed.

Kate looked back at Tanner. "I don't guess we're going to get much more tonight."

Tanner closed his book. "Not likely."

The doctor returned and Kate got up to meet him. "What's Mr. Hampton's status?"

He pointed toward the hallway. "Let's go out there."

Tanner and Kate obliged, and after sliding the curtain shut, the doctor turned to face them.

"He was pretty incoherent when they brought him in, but after a short time, the reality of his situation seemed to come into focus."

Kate's concern played across her face. "Will you keep him overnight?"

"Depends on how he feels in a couple hours. Right now, I'd say probably."

Kate nodded. "Thanks, Doc."

"Of course."

The doctor left to see to other patients.

Kate turned to her partner. "So, what do you think?"

"I want to check his alibi. If it holds up, I'd say he is unlikely to be our guy."

"Works for me. You're the chauffeur, so let's go."

"Should we wait for the business office to open in the morning?"

She grunted. "Have you ever seen Monday morning traffic at DIA?"

"Good point." He laughed. "Get in the car, Kate. I'm not gonna wait forever."

She glared at him briefly. "Careful, Rookie!"

For the second time that evening, he wasn't sure if she was joking.

Denver International Airport
8500 Peña Boulevard
Northeast Denver
11:55 p.m.

Denver International Airport was not the busiest airport in the nation, but it was the largest in area. Covering nearly fifty-three square miles, the three concourses were connected by buses, shuttles, and an underground rail.

DIA was best known for the Jeppesen Terminal, the huge, white, teepee-like structures that were supposed to remind visitors of snow-capped mountains. Most folks thought they were meant to represent teepees of the Native Americans who once inhabited the area. Whichever the design was meant to be, it had become iconic.

As Kate had predicted, the middle of the night provided a much-less-difficult entrance to the expansive complex. They

parked in the east lot and made their way to
the Southwest Airlines office.

A young man with short, curly hair
and olive skin was alone at the baggage
check-in. Clad in the latest Southwest
uniform of gray slacks and a red, button-
down shirt, he sported a nametag that
identified him as Bryce. He smiled brightly
as they approached.

"Can I help you?"

Kate held up her badge. "Good
evening. I'm Detective Walker, and this is
my partner, Detective Austin. We need some
information."

His smile shrank slightly but didn't
disappear completely—a skill Tanner
assumed came with practice. The clerk
looked over his shoulder then back at them.

"What kind of information?"

"We need to verify a pilot's schedule."

"Well, all the flight crew scheduling is
done out of our operations center in Dallas."

Kate kept her own practiced smile in
place. "What about here? Who do pilots
check in with when they arrive?"

The clerk looked over his shoulder
again, as if he expected someone any
minute. "They use the crew room, which has
computers for them to log on to and
mailboxes for them to check. I don't have
access to that area."

"Is there anyone here who does?"

"Not at the moment. We don't have any flights leaving for several hours."

Kate pointed over his shoulder. "Why do you keep looking behind you?"

"My replacement was due at midnight. They're late."

Tanner pulled out his pad. "Do you have the number for the Dallas operations center?"

Bryce nodded. "Wait here. I'll be back in a second."

Kate turned to Tanner. "What are you thinking?"

"Maybe we can get a printout faxed to us and avoid another trip out here."

"Makes sense."

True to his word, Bryce returned quickly with a business card.

"It's an eight hundred number."

Tanner took the card. "Thanks. And I hope your relief shows up soon."

Bryce's tension eased. "Yeah, me, too!"

Back at the car, Tanner suggested they call it a night. "There's not much to do until the autopsy."

Kate nodded. "True. Let's get some rest!"

"Yes, ma'am."

35

DENVER HOMICIDE

Monday, April 6

Office of the Medical Examiner
686 Bannock Street
Lincoln Park District
Southwest of Downtown Denver
6:45 a.m.

The domain of the Denver medical examiner, and all the death investigations she oversaw, was ironically situated inside the Denver Health Administration building. To Tanner, it was odd, at best and dumb, at worst, to put the coroner's office within the confines of the city health center.

Kate had called early that morning to advise him the autopsy on Carole Hampton was to be performed at seven o'clock and to ask if he was interested in attending with her. Interested might not have been the first word that came to him at just past 5:00 a.m., but he wasn't about to let her go alone. An hour later, she'd picked him up.

Though it was early, both Tanner and his partner had managed to catch a few hours of sleep. The same could not be said for Dana McCloud. They found her in her office putting on her lab coat. The mystery was, at least to Tanner, that she still managed to look fresher and more alert than either he or Kate did.

"Good morning, Detectives."

Kate nodded while Tanner looked around, trying to remember where the coffee pot was kept.

Dana smiled. "Ready for a show?"

Kate grinned. "Always happy to watch your handiwork, Dana."

"Even this early?"

"I won't deny I prefer afternoon autopsies."

Dana looked over at Tanner. "Lose something?"

"Coffee?"

Dana pointed toward the hallway. "Turn right. In the breakroom."

He turned to Kate. "Want some?"

"Please. I'll meet you in the observatory."

"Okay."

Just a few minutes later, Tanner entered the overhead observatory. His

38

partner was the only occupant. "Here's your coffee."

Kate accepted it without turning from the large glass window. "Thanks."

Tanner opted to remain standing. "Did I miss anything?"

"Just photos and the rape kit. Dana said it doesn't appear Mrs. Hampton was assaulted."

"Well, that removes one possible motive."

The coroner had a male tech, also dressed in a surgical robe, gloves, mask, and goggles, to assist her. He handed a scalpel to Dana. Starting at the shoulders, she made the familiar Y-shaped incision, stopping just above the groin.

Blood doesn't pump from a dead body, so the incision was much less messy than it would have been on a living person. After death, blood and other fluids only left the body when gravity assisted them. The result was a slightly less gory scene than one would expect when a body was opened up.

Despite that, Tanner always found the exposing of the inner organs to be the toughest part. His partner had no similar reservations that he could detect. Her eyes remained glued to the process the entire time. He sipped his coffee and tried to listen rather than watch. The mic over the table was recording Dana's observations, as well as piping them into the observatory.

All the organs were examined and weighed, and trauma was searched for but not found. Carole Hampton appeared to have been in good health—except for her head.

Dana made a semi-circular cut from in front of one ear, across the top of the skull, to in front of the other ear. Grasping the skin, she peeled it forward to expose the front of the cranium, all the while talking.

"Peeling back of skull covering reveals two holes in frontal bone, roughly a half-inch apart and approximately the same size."

She pulled the scalp all the way back and uncovered the rear of the skull.

"No trauma or sign of exit wounds present in either the parietal or occipital bones."

The tech handed his boss a bone saw, and after looking up at an x-ray on the lighted wall screen, she began to remove the cranium. To Tanner, it was surprising that this part didn't bother him. Most people he told about autopsies were freaked out by bone saws.

Dana continued. "Removal of the bone structure around the wound revealed two projectiles."

The assistant handed Dana a pair of oversized tweezers, and she extracted one bullet and then the other. She dropped them into a metal pan held out by the tech, each slug clinking with the same "ting" heard on television crime shows.

Kate leaned forward and pushed the observatory microphone button. "Can you tell what caliber, Dana?"

Without looking up, Dana pushed the bullets around in the bowl with a gloved finger then spoke into the mic. "Small, appear to be twenty-fives."

"Thanks."

Dana waved absently, focusing on the task of removing the brain. Kate and Tanner had what they needed for now and headed out.

The Delectable Egg
1642 Market Street
Downtown Denver
8:15 a.m.

Not long after joining the Denver Police Department, Kate discovered The

Delectable Egg. Like her, it was unpretentious, plain, and comfortable. The food was great, and it had quickly become her favorite breakfast spot. She found a space in the parking lot across the street from the restaurant and pulled in.

She and Tanner were now familiar to the servers, and it didn't take long for the two of them to be led to a table. The food was always good, but the staff was what brought Kate back time and time again. Always attentive, but never overbearing. She liked her space, and they respected that.

Tanner ordered a basic breakfast while Kate went with eggs benedict. Their meals were delivered quickly, and they ate in silence.

Tanner finished first. "What's up with you?"

Kate looked up, surprised by the question.

"What do you mean?"

He sipped his coffee, watching her over the rim of his mug. "I may not have been a detective for the half-century you have…"

Her eyes widened. "Watch it!"

He grinned. "But I can sense when my partner has something on her mind."

She ate the last of her eggs then pushed the plate away from her. She hadn't planned on telling him until after she'd informed the lieutenant and had to admit she was impressed with Tanner's perception.

"If I tell you, it has to stay between us."

"Of course."

"I've put in for a transfer out of Homicide."

Tanner stared at her as if he hadn't heard. His expression remained blank, his eyes guarded. After nearly a minute of digesting the news, he sat back in his seat.

Before he could respond, their waitress arrived.

"Can I take these plates out of your way?"

Tanner didn't answer, so Kate nodded. "Please, and can we get some more coffee?"

"Sure."

When she was gone, Kate allowed an uncomfortable smirk across her face.

"Aren't you going to say something? I thought you'd be surprised."

Tanner sighed.

"Oh, I'd say surprised is an understatement. Shocked, stunned, or maybe even flabbergasted would do better. Of all the things I would've guessed you were about to tell me, that would be the last one."

"Why? I mean, I know I haven't given any indication, but why so over-the-top?"

She sensed he was searching for words. Finally, he sat forward, shaking his head.

"Let's see. First thing that occurs to me is you're nuts. I've watched you for what, six months now, and you're a natural detective. You get things with your gut that no one else would perceive."

Fresh coffee arrived, and he waited while the cups were topped off before continuing.

"But more than that, you seem to thrive on the challenge. Putting the pieces together, solving the equation, and then locking up the perp are what you're about."

She dumped some powdered creamer in her cup and absentmindedly swished her spoon around. "That's the point, I guess."

"What is?"

"Solving murders is what I'm about, but that's not enough. I'll be retiring in a year or two, and then what? I'm not sure I want a long string of bodies to be all I have to remember of my time on the force."

Tanner was watching her intently, his eyes revealing the skepticism he was feeling.

"It's not me, is it?"

Bewildered, she cocked her head to one side.

"You?"

It dawned on her what he meant.

"No... absolutely not. This has nothing to do with you or any other partner I've had."

He raised an eyebrow. "Are you sure? I wouldn't want to be responsible..."

She dismissed him with a wave.

"Don't be ridiculous. This has nothing to do with you, and if it did, I would just ask you to be reassigned."

He gave a lopsided grin. "Thanks... I guess."

She laughed. "You're a good partner, and you'll be a very good detective, but let me give you a piece of advice."

"Okay—shoot."

"If the job swallows you, get out."

"Swallows me?"

She shrugged. "I don't know how else to describe it. The cases become all you can think about, all you care about, all that matters. It's like falling into a hole, and climbing out can be very difficult."

His smile disappeared. "Is that what this is about?"

"No, but I've been there. Some detectives never make it out. The job steals their soul."

A silence filled the space between them, and Kate suddenly felt the need to clarify.

"Look at it this way; being a homicide detective is all the things you imagine — and more — but it's still a job. Make sure it remains that and doesn't become your life."

He nodded slowly. "Thanks, Kate."

"No problem, and remember, not a word to anyone about this."

"Got it."

Denver Police Department District 2 Precinct Holly Street 9:30 a.m.

Tanner sat down at his desk and pulled out the business card the Southwest Airlines employee had given him. Dialing the eight hundred number, he found himself connected to a real person.

"Operations Coordination Center. This is Julie."

"Hi, Julie. My name is Detective Austin with the Denver PD. I'm investigating a case here and need some information on one of your people."

"What kind of information, sir?"

"I need to confirm one of your pilot's schedules."

"Okay. Please hold, and I'll get you to someone who can help."

"Thank you."

He was on hold for probably six or seven minutes, then a male voice came on the phone.

"This is Mark Campbell, Senior Flight Scheduler. Who am I speaking with?"

"Mr. Campbell, my name is Detective Austin with the Denver PD."

"What can I help you with, Detective?"

"One of your pilots, Tom Hampton, is involved in a case I'm investigating. I need to verify his whereabouts last night."

"I see. Did he mention the route he flew?"

"Yes. He came in from Las Vegas."

Tanner picked up the tapping of computer keys coming through the phone. After just seconds, the scheduler found what he was looking for.

"He pulled back from the gate at McCarron in Las Vegas at 4:20 p.m. Denver time, and his flight took one hour, fifty-five minutes, with his arrival clocked in at 6:15 p.m."

Tanner made a note of the times. "Is the arrival time when he landed?"

"No, it's when he shuts off the engines."

"Thank you, sir. Could I get a paper copy of that?"

"Sure. I can fax it."

Tanner gave him the number and hung up.

He found Kate coming back from the bathroom. "I got the info on Tom Hampton's alibi."

"Okay. Does it check out?"

"Yes and no."

She grinned. "Perhaps you'd care to explain?"

"Well, Hampton said he got in to DIA around 6:45, and it took him about ninety minutes to get home, arriving there around 8:15, right?"

She nodded. "Sounds right."

"Except it doesn't match the time charts from the airline. According to the Operations Center, his flight arrived into Denver at 6:15. With the ninety minutes added that Hampton said it took him to get home, that puts him at the house by 7:45."

"Which means he was home within the window given by Dana as TOD."

"Exactly."

Kate reached over and picked up her phone. "You know the number to UCH?"

Tanner found it in his notepad. "Why are you calling there?"

"I want to see if Hampton is still there."

Ten minutes later, they were on the way to University Hospital.

University of Colorado Hospital
Room 623
Aurora, Colorado
10:45 a.m.

Kate tapped lightly on the door marked 623.

From inside came a groggy response. "Yeah?"

She pushed the door halfway open. "Mr. Hampton?"

"Yeah."

"It's Detective Walker. May I come in?"

"Yeah."

After pushing the door open completely, she entered the dimly lit room, followed by Tanner. A young man looked up from his perch in a chair by the window, his resemblance to Tom Hampton obvious. His navy suit indicated he worked in a professional capacity; Kate guessed attorney. She nodded a greeting then turned to Tom.

"How are you doing, Mr. Hampton?"

Propped up by a couple pillows, Hampton looked much as he did the night before. His eyes maintained a level of glassiness that made her unsure how much he was going to comprehend, and the sluggishness of his movements only served to increase her doubts.

"I'm here. They wouldn't let me go home."

"Did they say why?"

He attempted to make a wave of dismissal at their reasoning, but no explanation followed.

The man by the window stood. "His blood pressure was off the charts, and they couldn't slow his heartrate."

Tom gestured weakly toward the stranger. "Detective, this is my son."

Kate reached out a hand. "Nice to meet you. I'm Detective Walker, and that is my partner, Detective Austin."

"Michael Hampton. I got in late last night."

"I'm sorry for your loss."

"Thank you, but the truth is, I wasn't close to my stepmother. In fact, I didn't like her."

Tom scowled.

"Now is not the time, Michael."

Michael touched his father's hand.

"You're right, Dad. I'm sorry."

Out of the corner of her eye, Kate noticed Tanner take out his notebook as he sized up Michael. She turned her attention to Tom.

"Do you mind answering a few questions for us?"

"I'll try. Have you got any suspects?"

Kate was careful not to tip her hand. Suggesting that Hampton was the only one they had right then would not help get answers from him. Besides, a new one may have just shown up in the room. "We're working several angles. We're hoping you can help us with that."

"Okay."

"Had you noticed anything unusual in the days leading up to the attack?"

His effort to focus was obvious.

"Nah... not that I can remember."

"What about Carole? Did she mention anything?"

The impact of his wife's name was heartbreaking. His eyes moistened, and his gaze fell to look at the ring on his hand.

"If there was anything, she never mentioned it."

"Did she work?"

He shook his head wearily. "No. She took an early buyout last year when the airline cut staff."

Tanner moved closer to the end of the bed. "Mr. Hampton?"

"Tom is fine."

"Tom, what airline did your wife work for?"

"Southwest. Same as me."

"Did she leave on good terms with the company and her coworkers?"

Tom shrugged. "As far as I know. I never heard anyone at the airline say a bad thing about her, but then they wouldn't, would they? Not around me."

"No, probably not."

Kate leaned closer. "What about passengers? Did she have problems with anyone who traveled her route regularly?"

"Again, not that I know of."

She could see the questions were beginning to sap what little strength the man had.

"Just a couple more things, Tom. You mentioned you got into DIA from Vegas at

6:45. The flight record said you arrived at 6:15."

Almost like a switch had been thrown, his eyes cleared and brightened. "What?"

Though she sensed it was unnecessary, she repeated it anyway.

"The airline record says you arrived at 6:15, which would get you home around 7:45. Does that sound right to you?"

"No… I mean, yes. The airline records are not always right. I can only tell you what I remember."

"So, you're not one hundred percent which is correct?"

His expression turned dark. "I'm not sure about a lot of things right now, Detective."

Michael apparently shared his father's annoyance. "Perhaps you should wait until he feels better to ask these questions."

Kate forced a smile and stood. "Of course. I hope you feel better, and again, we're sorry for your loss."

Kate looked at Michael. "Could we speak to you out in the hall?"

Michael nodded then leaned over his father. "Be right back, Dad."

If the elder Mr. Hampton heard his son, he didn't respond.

Back in the hallway, Kate led Michael, followed by Tanner, down to a waiting room. It was empty, so they each took a seat around a small table. Kate still wore her smile, but she had her reservations about the man sitting opposite her.

She got right to the point. "You didn't like your stepmother. Can I ask why?"

Michael crossed his arms and leaned back in his chair. "Look, I know what I said in there came off as cold, but you have to understand the family history. Carole purposely worked to separate my father and me."

"For what reason?"

"I'd tell you to ask her, but obviously, that won't work. I'm not sure—money, I guess—but she never liked me. That I know. She would find any number of ways to keep my father and me from speaking."

"What money?"

"My mother's. She was a very wealthy woman when she passed away."

Tanner looked up from his notetaking. "How did she die?"

Michael sighed. "She was shot and killed during a robbery."

"Here in Denver?"

"No. Salt Lake City."

"Did they find the killer?"

"They put someone in jail. You'd have to ask the Salt Lake police if they think they got the killer."

Tanner and Kate exchanged looks. Kate leaned on the table, looking directly into Michael's eyes. "You sound unconvinced?"

"I have my own theory about what happened."

"Would you care to let us in on it?"

The man shook his head. "Not really. I don't see anything to be gained by opening up old wounds. It doesn't matter now."

Kate decided not to push. "Obviously, you don't live locally. Where are you from?"

"I'm the La Plata County Prosecutor. I live in Durango."

Kate had pegged him exactly.

"Is that where you were on the night Carole was killed?"

"It is. You can talk to my pastor. He'll verify I was at Easter services Sunday morning and helped set up the egg hunt that afternoon."

The alibi was not something Kate would have guessed.

"We'll do that. Thank you for your time."

When Michael was gone, she stared at Tanner. "What do you think?"

Tanner snorted. "About which one?"

"The son."

"If his alibi is good, there's no way he could be responsible."

"What about his story about his mother's murder?"

"I don't know what he thinks happened. My guess is he feels Carole Hampton had a hand in it, but who knows."

Kate nodded. "That was my feeling. What about Tom Hampton's answers?"

Tanner shrugged. "He could just be confused. People's memories are notoriously fragile."

"True, but that question got his full attention, didn't it?"

"It most certainly did. What now?"

She smiled. "You tell me?"

He dragged himself to his feet.

"What's the airport traffic like at midday?"

She laughed. "You're a detective. You figure it out."

Denver International Airport
8500 Peña Boulevard
1:25 p.m.

A drive-thru lunch and two hours in traffic finally ended with them parking at the baggage unload area next to the Southwest Airlines offices. If Carole Hampton had left an angry coworker or customer behind, they may have sought out their revenge.

Tanner stuck his blue light on the car's roof and left the flashers going.

"We better not be long."

Kate nodded. "Agreed. Let's go."

This time, when they approached the Southwest counter, multiple red shirts greeted them. Tanner showed his badge.

"I'm a detective with the Denver PD. Is there a manager about?"

The clerk, a young blonde in her mid-twenties, maintained her smile despite the badge. Tanner had to admit the airline employees were good at keeping that smile locked in place.

She held up her hand. "One sec."

She turned and went through a swinging door. In less than a minute, she returned.

"If you'll step around the corner there, Mr. Givens will meet you."

Tanner stared in the direction she pointed and spotted an inconspicuous door, gray with no window, bearing a small sign.

Southwest-Authorized Personnel Only.
He smiled at her. "Thank you."

Kate and Tanner, who was still holding his badge, walked down to the door. It opened just as they arrived. A man wearing gray slacks and a blue polo shirt nodded then waved them inside the office. Closing the door behind them, he finally turned to greet them.

"I'm Burt Givens, Operations Manager."

Tanner put away his badge. "Detective Austin, and this is my partner, Detective Walker."

"Nice to meet you. Please, follow me."

He led them down a short hallway and into a conference room.

"Please, have a seat. Would you like a cup of coffee?"

Tanner held up his hand.

"No, thank you. In fact, our parking spot has us on borrowed time."

Burt smiled. "I understand."

"We're here to ask about one of your former employees."

"Carole Hampton?"

"Yes. How did you know?"

Burt's mood turned melancholy.

"We heard this morning. Word gets around, you know."

Kate had stood leaning against the wall by the door, her arms crossed. "Did you know Mr. and Mrs. Hampton well?"

"Yeah, I guess. As well as you can know any coworker. I liked them both."

"We understand Carole Hampton took an early buyout. Is that correct?"

"Yeah. It was a good deal at a great time for her. She had other interests she wanted to pursue."

Kate raised an eyebrow. "Oh? Anything in particular?"

Burt shrugged. "I know she was passionate about the arts."

"The arts?"

"Yeah, painting and such."

Tanner had his pad out and made the notation. "Don't crews tend to fly together?"

"Yeah, most of the time."

"How did she get along with her regular coworkers?"

"Fine. I never heard of any trouble."

"Was there anyone not part of her crew that she didn't get along with?"

"No. At least, she never filed a grievance that I'm aware of."

Frustrated, Tanner glanced at his watch. The trip out there had done them very little good. "Thank you for your time, sir."

"Not at all."

Kate and Tanner shook Burt's hand then headed back to the car. The blue light seemed to have done its job, which meant their vehicle had not been towed. They were soon on their way.

Tanner glanced at Kate. "What do you think about the airline connection to the murder?"

Her reaction was decidedly negative. "I find it unlikely that someone had it out for her but waited a year to act on it."

"I have to agree. I still don't like the fuzziness of Tom Hampton's timeline, though."

"That makes two of us."

Denver Police Department
District 2 Precinct
Holly Street
3:20 p.m.

When they arrived back at the precinct, both detectives found a report waiting for them on their desk. Tanner had a manila envelope marked *Forensics: Walker*.

60

He pulled out a thick sheaf of papers divided into several sections by paperclips. The top sheet was a summary.

<u>Forensic Report on Hampton Residence.</u>
<u>4699 Granby Way.</u>

No unidentified fingerprints in home or in vehicles.
Blood belonged to victim.
No unidentified hairs found on bedspread, carpet, clothing, or in either vehicle.
No biological material tested.
GSR test from victim and submitted sample from Mr. Hampton—both negative.

<u>Items brought to lab for processing:</u>

Make-up bench.
Victim's shirt (found on floor)
Victim's clothing found on body— includes skirt and panties.
Bedspread from master bedroom
Gunshot Residue Swabs—Taken at scene—Sample from Thomas Hampton, spouse of victim.
2015 Mercedes coupe
2014 Cadillac CTS

Slugs removed from body have been identified as .25 caliber, with rifling characteristics present on one slug. No comparison weapon at this time.

Tanner moved on to the next sheaf of papers.

<u>Autopsy Results: Carole Hampton</u>

* *Victim in overall good health.*
* *Means of death—Gunshot trauma to brain.*
* *Mode of death—.25 caliber.*
* *Manner of death—Homicide.*

No biological material found under nails or in vaginal swab. Victim did not have signs of sexual trauma. Only injuries were as a result of gunshot wounds.

He skipped over the rest.
"What's that?" Looking over his shoulder was Kate.
He sighed. "Forensic report. Pretty much a big goose egg as far as new information."
"Wanna trade?"
"What have you got?"
"Neighborhood canvas."
"Oh? Anything interesting?"

She dropped the folder on top of the forensic files.

"I'll tell you what. I'll drive, and you can read. Fill me in on the forensic report first, then look over the canvas interviews."

He pushed his chair back from his desk.

"Yes, ma'am."

Home of Nettie Tiller
Montbello Neighborhood
Northeast Denver
4:15 p.m.

There were only two canvas reports of any interest. The first came from the house across the street from the Hampton residence.

Kate knocked on the door, but when no answer came, she pushed the bell. A long, low, resonating bell, from deep in the home, came back to them. A minute more and the door cracked open enough for a small voice to be heard.

"Yes?"

Kate squinted at the opening and held up her badge. "Good afternoon. My name is Detective Walker. Can I speak with you for a minute?"

"Who's he?"

"That's my partner, Detective Austin." Tanner smiled broadly. "Hi."

The door opened another few inches.

"Hold the badge closer, please."

Kate obliged.

After just a second, the door opened completely to reveal a tiny woman with white hair and large spectacles.

"You must be here about Mrs. Hampton." Her voice trembled.

Kate put away her badge. "Yes, ma'am. Do you mind talking to us?"

She stepped back to let them in. "No. The officer I talked to yesterday told me to expect you. Please, come in."

Once they were inside, the woman finally managed a smile.

"I'm sorry about keeping you outside, but I've been scared ever since what happened to Carole."

Kate removed her sunglasses.

"It's quite all right. I think you're correct to be cautious."

The elderly woman smoothed some imaginary wrinkles on the white-and-red-floral housedress she wore. "Where are my manners? Would you like to sit down?"

Kate smiled. "That would be nice."

The elderly woman guided them into a sitting room off the side of the hallway. Kate followed and accepted the small tan armchair offered. Tanner sat in the matching chair next to her and took out his notepad.

Their hostess sat opposite them on a large, antique divan, covered in a worn brown fabric that featured large orange mums on the back.

"My name is Nettie Tiller."

The oversized sofa seemed to swallow Nettie as she sat alone on the middle cushion, her hands folded in her lap, her gaze on the floor.

A large china hutch and an oversized buffet, much like the ones Kate's grandmother had, took up an entire wall at the far end of the room. Opposite the front window was a small fireplace and above it, a portrait.

Kate pointed at the picture. "Is that you, Nettie?"

The little woman seemed startled by the question, almost as if she'd forgotten Kate and Tanner were there.

"Oh…oh, yes. That's my husband Earl. He surprised me on our fiftieth anniversary with a picture portrait. Then he took the photo to someone who made a painting of it."

Kate couldn't imagine a love that lasted so long. Her relationships never made it to *one* year. She envied the couple's affection for each other, somehow captured by the artist.

"It's beautiful."

"Thank you. Earl passed five years ago this June."

"I'm sorry."

A brief lull in the conversation allowed Tanner to redirect things. "Mrs. Tiller..."

"Nettie, please."

"Nettie. Did you know Mr. and Mrs. Hampton well?"

"Just as a neighbor. We would chat if we got the mail at the same time, that sort of thing."

"Did you ever notice any problems between them?"

"No, not that I can remember. They were always cordial and warm."

"In the interview with the officer, you mentioned seeing a man walking away from the Hampton's home on the night Mrs. Hampton was killed. Do you remember what time that was?"

"Well, let's see. The news was over, Jeopardy was over, and I think Wheel had just ended."

Tanner raised an eyebrow. "Wheel?"

Kate smiled. "Wheel of Fortune."

Nettie grinned. "I love that Vanna White."

Apparently, game shows weren't his thing. "So, what time would that be?"

"Eight, maybe a little before."

"Did you recognize the man?"

"No."

Tanner looked up. "Could you describe him?"

"I gave a description to the officer when he was here."

Kate smiled. "Would you mind doing it again, just for us?" Kate's voice was soothing.

Nettie nodded, then scrunched her forehead and closed her eyes in an apparent effort to see the man again.

"Tall, not white, but not black. Short hair, light in color, but not blond."

Tanner's pen moved across his pad. "What about clothing?"

Nettie's eyes reopened. "Long, dark pants, but not blue jeans. A black jacket, but not a heavy coat."

Kate didn't know whether to cry at the plainness of the description or laugh at the manner in which it was delivered.

"Nettie, do you think you could describe him to a sketch artist?"

Nettie shook her head. "Oh, I don't think so. I just can't be sure enough of what I saw. These are old eyes, you know."

Kate nodded. "This man. What direction was he heading?"

"South—toward Andrews Avenue."

Kate sensed there wasn't any point in quizzing Nettie further, so she stood, joined by Tanner.

"You've been very helpful."

Nettie remained seated, seemingly worn out by the short visit. Kate handed her a business card.

"Will you call me if you think of anything else?"

"Of course."

"Thank you. We'll let ourselves out."

Nettie rose slowly from her seat. "I'll go with you. I want to lock the door."

Back in their car, Tanner was staring at his notes. "The time she gives doesn't clear Tom Hampton, but it doesn't make sense he would be on foot."

"No, unless it was pre-planned to leave his car elsewhere." Kate smiled at him. "What do you make of the description?"

Tanner chuckled. "We know what he's not. He's not black, not white, not wearing blue jeans, and not wearing a heavy jacket."

Kate laughed. "She's very nice, but I don't guess her information will help much. Where next?"

He pointed over his shoulder. "That way."

"Okay. Let's go."

Home of Kenneth Blackwell
Montbello Neighborhood
Northeast Denver
5:05 p.m.

Only four doors down and a few minutes later, they were waiting for an answer at a large, gothic-style, wooden door. Unlike their experience at Nettie Tiller's home, their first knock here drew a response, and a tall, slender man in his forties opened the door.

"Can I help you?"

Kate held up her badge. "My name is Detective Walker, and this is my partner, Detective Austin. May we have a few minutes of your time?"

"What's this about?"

"We're investigating the murder of Carole Hampton. Your name came up on one of the neighborhood interviews."

"Oh..."

The brief hesitation didn't go unnoticed. Kate raised an eyebrow "Is this a bad time?"

"No, it's fine. Come in."

The interior of Kenneth Blackwell's home couldn't have been more different from Nettie Tiller's place. Where she had antique pieces, his were modern. Where she had bold colors, he had black, white, and stainless steel. Kate preferred the warmth of Nettie's.

They walked single file down a hallway to the kitchen, another room of stainless steel and white. Blackwell pulled out a chair and sat at the breakfast bar. He didn't offer a seat to Kate and Tanner.

"What is it you needed to know?"

Kate met his stare, trying to size up the level of truth she might expect from the man. She wasn't expecting much.

"We understand you were friends with the couple."

His brown, button-front shirt was open at the collar to reveal his tan, which to Kate bore the telltale signs of being sprayed on. His khaki slacks, beige sandals, and brown hair that swept back from his forehead gave

70

him a youthful look. The silver stud that sparkled from his left ear suggested college professor to Kate.

"No, not the couple, just Carole. I never met Tom."

"I see. How did you come to meet Mrs. Hampton?"

"She was in an art class of mine at the university."

Kate smiled inwardly. *Nailed him.*

"University?"

"Rocky Mountain College of Art. I'm an instructor there."

Tanner jotted it down. "Was this class still going on?"

"Yes. There are two weeks left in the semester."

Kate's creepy meter was off the scale with this guy. "How would you describe your connection to Mrs. Hampton?"

"We were friends."

"So, not just an instructor-student relationship?"

"It began as that, of course, but we developed a friendship."

"Was it a close friendship?"

"I'd say so. We had a lot of things in common."

"Do you develop close relationships with all your students?"

Blackwell stared at her for a long time. "I'm not sure I understand your point."

"Let me restate it then. Is it common for you to develop similar friendships with your students?"

"Common, no. But it does happen on occasion."

Kate pushed harder. "How would you describe the closeness of this relationship with *Mrs.* Hampton?"

"What do you mean?"

"Well, would you call it casual, personal...intimate?"

Blackwell eyes darkened and his voice became tinged with anger. "I don't like your suggestion, Detective."

Kate remained unphased.

"So it wasn't intimate?"

"We were friends. I'm sure you understand the term *friend*, don't you, Detective."

"Of course. When was the last time you saw Carole Hampton?"

"The night before her death. She was at class that Saturday night."

"Where were you on the night Carole Hampton was killed?"

"Here. I was home alone." Blackwell's face had flushed, and contempt dripped from every word.

"Anybody able to vouch for that?"

"I'm divorced. My ex-wife and kids live in Colorado Springs, so instead of seeing them for Easter, I received a phone call."

"What time was this call?"

"I talked to them until nearly seven thirty that night."

Her questions were rapid fire, intended to throw him off balance. "And what did you do after that?"

"Watched some TV before going to bed."

"What time did you go to bed?"

"I don't know. Ten o'clock, maybe."

Kate ended the interview as abruptly as it had started.

"Thank you, Mr. Blackwell. We'll see ourselves out."

She flashed Tanner a satisfied smile as they left the home.

DENVER HOMICIDE

<u>Tuesday, April 7</u>

Denver Police Department
District 2 Precinct
Holly Street
8:10 a.m.

Tanner made it his first task the next morning to verify the alibi they'd received from the younger Mr. Hampton. It had taken just minutes to reach someone at the church office.

Sure enough, Michael Hampton had been at church services on Sunday, and helped set-up the egg hunt later that day. With slightly more than three hundred miles between Durango and Denver, it was clear Michael was not their killer.

Tanner had just hung up when his phone rang. "This is Detective Austin."

"Good morning, Detective. My name is Officer Pope."

"Morning, Officer. What can I do for you?"

"I understand you're working the Carole Hampton case."

"That's right. Why?"

"I was the responding officer to the Carole Hampton scene, and I realized there may have been something I failed to mention in my report."

The officer now had Tanner's full attention. "What is this something?"

"Well, it may be nothing, but…"

Tanner sensed an underlying nervousness in the officer's speech and thought he might know why.

"Officer Pope… What's your first name?"

"Eric."

"Listen, Eric, I'm not concerned if you made an error in judgment at the scene or forgot something in a report. My only concern is catching the S.O.B. who killed Carole Hampton. Do we understand each other?"

"Yes, sir. Thank you."

"So what is it you wanted to share?"

"When I was having my initial conversation with Mr. Hampton, a man showed up on the scene and started asking about Carole Hampton. I didn't answer his questions and had him removed to outside the perimeter. I didn't think much of it until I asked Tom Hampton if he knew the man. Mr. Hampton said no."

Tanner was taking notes. "Did the man say anything to Tom Hampton?"

"No, in fact, he didn't seem to notice Mr. Hampton at all. His only concern was Mrs. Hampton."

"What time was this?"

"About nine fifteen, I think."

"Did the man say where he lived?"

"A few doors down."

Tanner's adrenaline surged.

"What about a name? Did he give you a name?"

"Ken. I didn't get a last name, and, unfortunately, I never followed up."

Ken from a few doors down. Tanner subconsciously crossed his fingers. "Can you describe him?"

"Brown hair, tall, slender. Oh, and he was tanned, which I found odd for this time of year."

That seals it. It has to be Blackwell.

"Eric?"

"Yes."

"Thanks for calling. Let me know if you think of anything else."

"Yes, sir."

Kate walked up just as Tanner put down the phone. Still charged up by the conversation, he spun in his chair.

"Guess what?"

Kate stopped, looked behind her, then turned and touched her chest. "Me?"

Tanner laughed. "Yes, you! Who else would I be talking to?"

She shrugged. "I don't know. Your imaginary friend?"

Tanner's smile disappeared. "Hey, you leave him out of this!"

It was Kate's turn to laugh. "Fair enough. What have you got?"

He filled her in on the conversation with Eric Pope and then waited for her reaction. She sat down at her desk and steepled her hands in front of her. "Hmmm."

"Hmmm? That's it? Shouldn't we go pick him up and grill him some more?"

"We could do that."

"But?"

"But I want to be in as strong a position as possible if we are going to confront him with new information."

Tanner realized this was one of those times to listen and learn. "Okay. So?"

"So, let's get his phone records and verify his alibi phone call to Colorado Springs. Then let's take a ride out to where he teaches and see what we can learn from his coworkers."

Tanner sighed. "Well, that could work, too."

She smiled. "Just a few suggestions, mind you."

"Whatever!" He laughed. "I'll drive, but that's just a suggestion, mind you."

"And a good one, at that."

****

It took another hour to get the subpoena filed for Kenneth Blackwell's phone records, but by nine thirty, they were on the road.

Tanner briefed her on his earlier phone call to Durango, which essentially cleared Michael Hampton. Afterward, the conversation lagged, and as he drove, Tanner's mind wandered to a topic that had troubled him since he found out.

"What will you do?"

Kate lifted an eyebrow. "I'm sorry?"

"You mentioned retirement. What will you do?"

She grinned. "Oh, that. Well, I'm not sure. Being a cop is all I've ever done, all I've ever wanted to do."

79

"Sure, I get it. But you must have some idea for after you're done."

"You mean like lying on a beach and enjoying the ocean breeze while sipping drinks with little umbrellas in them?"

He laughed. "Yeah, like that."

"Not for me. I might open a tiki bar that *serves* those drinks on a beach somewhere."

"That sounds like fun."

"Yeah, but I don't know. I lived my whole life in Colorado, and there isn't much call for tiki bars here."

"Nor are there many ocean breezes, either!"

She laughed. "Valid point!"

They pulled off I-70, known in the city as West Colfax, onto Pierce Street.

Tanner glanced at Kate. "You know, a woman with your skills could always land a job as a bank security officer."

She scowled at him. "Yeah, and if you came in, I'd shoot you on the spot."

He held his hands up in defeat. "Okay, okay. No security guard gig for you."

She turned serious. "Don't forget. You promised to keep this between us for now."

"I won't forget."

But he still didn't understand it.

JOHN C. DALGLISH

Colorado College of Art &
Design
Pierce Street
West Denver
10:15 a.m.

The sprawling campus of Colorado College revolved around a long stretch of grass that ran down the center of the quad. Lining each side of this stadium-sized greenery were multiple redbrick buildings that resembled old, country courthouses.

It would be almost idyllic if the grass was green, but that wouldn't be the case for another month or so. Instead, Tanner found the common area depressing. Everything was brown; brown lawn, brown trees, brown bushes. Then again, at least they weren't snow covered.

Kate was walking just ahead of him as they approached the circular driveway in front of the college office and was first to spot the lawn art.

"What do you make of that, Tanner?"

"Some sort of garden art, I guess. Looks like they might plant flowers beneath it."

"You're suggesting that's art?"

Tanner laughed. "It does look like half a soccer ball made out of steel. I'm sure it represents something."

"It reminds me of the jungle gym at the park near where I grew up."

Tanner pointed at the sign next to the structure. *Keep Off.*

"Well, this one they don't want you climbing on."

They moved around the artwork and up a set of concrete steps leading to the campus headquarters. Tanner had his badge out already, expecting to meet security as soon as they entered, but no one greeted them.

The entrance area was a large rotunda with a round, vaulted ceiling. Their shoes made clicking sounds on the marble floor tiles. A glass door to their left, one of four exits leading away from the rotunda, was marked "administration."

Tanner tapped Kate's shoulder. "Over there."

Kate turned, spotted the door, and led the way.

On the other side of the door, they found a different world from the quiet entryway. Noise cascaded over them from multiple sources, including phone's ringing, keyboards being tapped, numerous conversations, and copy machines spitting out sheets of paper. The office was also brightly lit, in contrast to the subdued lighting of the rotunda.

A dark-haired woman in her mid-forties looked up as they entered, pushing the wire-frame glasses that had slipped down her nose back up to their proper position. "May I help you?"

Tanner held out his badge. "Yes, thank you. I'm Detective Austin with the Denver PD, and this is my partner, Detective Walker."

"Good morning. Is there a problem?"

"No, not exactly. We need some information."

She pushed her glasses up again. "Well, you probably want our security office. It's across the rotunda from here."

Tanner tucked away his badge and smiled. "We may stop over there later, but right now, we'd like to speak with someone about one of your professors."

"I see. May I ask who?"

"Ken Blackwell."

A flash of recognition was quickly shielded by her hand repeating its eyewear chore.

"You need to talk with Elizabeth Cowling. She's in charge of the art department."

"Is she in?"

"Let me check." The clerk lifted a phone, punched in three numbers, and waited.

"Hi, Elizabeth. This is Nancy. I have a couple detectives here who would like to ask you a few questions." A brief pause was followed by a headshake. "No, not about you. About Ken Blackwell."

She followed a second pause with a nod. "Very well. I'll send them up."

Nancy hung up and pointed toward the entryway.

"Go back out our door, then turn left. The staircase will take you up to the second floor. Mrs. Cowling's office is immediately on your right."

Tanner thanked her then turned to inform Kate, but she was already on her way out the door.

The winding concrete staircase, larger and more elaborate than the one they'd climbed to enter the building, deposited them on the second floor. Kate spotted the office, and Tanner followed her.

They entered a very small room with no waiting area. The space was filled primarily by a large, wooden desk, which was surrounded on all sides by floor-to-ceiling bookshelves. Tanner noted the lack of a window and a vague odor of musty books.

A woman in her late fifties stood and extended her hand. Her hair was tied up in a bun and showed signs of once being a deep red but now had faded to an awkward orange. She was trim and carried herself with assurance.

"I'm Elizabeth Cowley, Dean of the Art Department."

She shook hands with Kate, then Tanner, before gesturing toward the two chairs in front of her desk.

"Please, make yourselves comfortable." She reseated herself and waited.

Kate smiled. "I'm Detective Walker. This is my partner, Detective Austin."

The dean focused on Kate.

"Nancy said you were here about Ken. What is it this time?"

Kate flashed a glance at Tanner before continuing. "So, if that was the case, it wouldn't be the first time?"

"No, but don't get me wrong—Ken is not a bad guy—he's just a pain in the butt, at least for me."

"Why is that?"

The dean's eyebrows knitted together, as if she was concerned she may be saying too much. "I'm sorry, but is there something in particular you needed to ask about?"

"Yes. We're looking to verify a few things about Mr. Blackwell."

"Such as?"

"Ken Blackwell is not married, correct?"

The dean shook her head. "Not since before he came here."

"And when was that?"

"About six years ago.

"Has Ken Blackwell been known to see any of his students romantically?"

The dean's teeth clenched, and she seemed to take a long time before her answer would come out. "Why?"

Kate sensed blood in the water. "Mrs. Cowley, we're investigating a murder. Your instructor happens to be a person of interest in that crime."

Tanner was certain he could hear the woman's teeth grinding now. He watched as the two women stared at each other. Finally, Cowley got her jaw to function.

"When I said Ken was a pain, I didn't mean to suggest he was capable of something like that."

Kate's inner bulldog would not be dissuaded. "Of course not, but you didn't answer my question. Does Ken Blackwell date his students?"

"On occasion."

"Are any of these students married?"

"I can't say for sure."

"Can't or won't?"

Colleges, and college deans, in particular, rely on their reputations...almost like a kind of currency. Cowley apparently sensed hers was about to get muddied.

"Is there anything else, Detective?"

"Do you know if Ken Blackwell was having a relationship with student Carole Hampton?"

"I do not." The dean's voice was now more of a hiss.

"Is there anyone who might know?"

"I'm afraid that would be outside of my area of responsibility."

Kate stared at Cowley for another moment then stood. Tanner was on his feet instantly and first to the door. He was ready to go.

But Kate hesitated. "One more thing, Mrs. Cowley. Did you and Ken Blackwell ever have an intimate relationship?"

Tanner stopped, not quite believing his ears. When he turned around, the dean was glaring at his partner.

"I will not dignify that with an answer!"

Kate nodded, apparently satisfied with some conclusion she'd drawn on her own.

"Okay. Thank you for your time."

As Kate came toward Tanner, she winked at him and said, "Let's go."

They didn't speak until they were back outside and walking to the car. Tanner was shaking his head.

"Man, you'll ask anything. What was that about? Were you just trying to piss her off?"

Kate laughed. "It worked, didn't it? She was about to come unglued."

"Sure, but why push her buttons?"

"Well, if Blackwell runs around with his students, then we want to know if it matters whether they're married or not."

"Why?"

"Well, let's say he only dates younger co-eds and not married women. That would lead us to believe a relationship between him and Carole Hampton was unlikely. But if he had no such inclination, then he would be near the top of our suspect list, correct?"

"Makes sense."

"So, when *Mrs.* Cowley refused to answer the question about married women, I took a stab in the dark. What do you think?"

"If I were a betting man, which I am, I'd say there was history between Blackwell and Dean Cowley."

"I think that would be a good bet. So, is it possible Blackwell and Carole Hampton were seeing each other?"

"Sure, but that doesn't mean he killed her."

"Nope, and his phone records may give him an alibi. But what if Tom Hampton knew his wife was cheating?"

Tanner stopped in his tracks. "That would be motive—for Tom."

"Precisely."

Tanner regained his pace, quicker now. "That is sneaky. You should do this for a living."

"Thanks, I think."

"So what now?"

"Now we check Mr. Blackwell's alibi, then make another visit to his home."

"Shouldn't we eat first?"

Kate laughed. "Hungry again? How do you stay trim?"

"Simple. If I get fat before the wedding, Laura will kill me. It's called the fear diet."

Denver Police Department
District 2 Precinct
Holly Street
12:30 p.m.

Kenneth Blackwell's phone records were on Kate's desk when she got back to the station. Before even sitting down, she picked up the thick pile of papers and scanned through multiple pages. Calls between Blackwell and Carole Hampton were frequent, but she expected that.

Continuing to scan, she was near the bottom of the pile before finally finding what she was after. Calls made and received on Easter Sunday. She ran her finger quickly down the page; the call from Colorado Springs stuck out.

Tanner came up behind her. "I got a message from UCH saying Tom Hampton had been released. Are those Blackwell's phone records?"

She nodded and handed him the page. "The call with his kids starts at six thirty-three Sunday evening and ends at seven-oh-two."

"Well, that fits with his alibi."

"Sort of. He claimed he was on the phone until nearly seven thirty."

Tanner handed the sheet back.

"The coroner placed Carole Hampton's TOD at between 6:00 and 8:00. That leaves him an hour."

"Yeah, and he only lives a few houses away. Also, he said he watched TV then went to bed around ten. He failed to mention his visit to the crime scene around nine-fifteen."

Kate turned and headed for the door, never having taken off her jacket.

"Let's go talk to Mr. Blackwell."

"Right behind you."

Home of Kenneth Blackwell
Montbello Neighborhood
Northeast Denver
4:25 p.m.

They arrived at Blackwell's home just as the garage door was opening. Kate turned into the driveway and blocked his path. Blackwell started to back up but must have caught sight of them just in time to avoid hitting their front bumper.

He jolted to a stop and stared into the rearview mirror. If he expected her to move, he was sadly mistaken.

Kate turned off the car and climbed out. Moving up by the driver's side, she indicated he should roll down his window. Tanner followed, coming up on the passenger side of Blackwell's silver Audi R8, a two-seat sports car.

Blackwell obliged but left the ten-cylinder motor running. When she spoke, he revved the engine, drowning out her first words. Rather than try again, she stepped back by the car and hooked her finger in his direction, indicating he should get out.

Tanner bent down to look in the passenger window and pointed toward Blackwell. "Out!"

Blackwell's options were get out or drive over them. He turned off the car and got out, closing the door behind him before leaning on the car.

He stared at Kate without speaking.

She smiled at him, apparently unmoved by his unwillingness to cooperate.

"Evening, Mr. Blackwell. Going somewhere?"

"I was. I have an evening class."

"If you don't mind answering a few questions, we won't keep you long."

Blackwell took a quick look around the neighborhood then headed for the still-open garage door. "In here."

Once inside, Blackwell leaned against the wall and waited.

Kate took out her notepad and read from it.

"In our original conversation, you said you talked to your kids until nearly seven-thirty; do you recall that?"

"Of course."

"Your phone records, however, do not support that. The phone call to Colorado Springs ended at seven-oh-two."

Blackwell shrugged, seemingly unmoved by the news. "I may have been mistaken. So what?"

"Were you mistaken when you forgot to mention visiting the Hampton residence?"

Blackwell froze, apparently lost for words.

Kate pressed him. "Our officer said you showed up there around nine-fifteen. You didn't think that was important to mention?"

His shoulders sagged. "Look, I didn't kill Carole. I saw all the police lights and was worried about her."

"Why just her and not Tom Hampton?"

He sighed. "Carole and I had a thing."

"A thing? You mean like a romantic thing?"

"You could say that."

"So, I could say you and Mrs. Hampton were having an affair?"

"Yes."

Some of the fight had gone out of Blackwell, and Kate began to suspect he actually had feelings for the dead woman. Of course, Kate couldn't care less about Blackwell's feelings, but she didn't want him to know that.

What she did care about was her next question. "Did Tom Hampton know about his wife's affair with you?"

Blackwell appeared to consider the question for a long time. Finally, he shook his head. "I don't think so. At least, Carole never said she thought he was on to her."

"You mean on to *us*?"

"Yeah, us. I don't think he knew about us, but I can't be sure."

Kate closed her notebook. "Thank you, Mr. Blackwell. We'll be getting out of your way now. If there's anything else, we'll be in touch."

Kate returned to the car, waited for Tanner to climb in, then pulled away. They

had gone several blocks before she said
anything.

"What do you think? Did he kill her?"

Tanner rubbed a hand across his chin,
scraping his afternoon stubble. "I don't think
so."

"What's your reasoning?"

"Well, despite the fact he has no
apparent moral compass, I think he cared for
Mrs. Hampton."

"So, it's your gut feeling, is that it?"

He shrugged. "I guess."

Kate glanced at him. "Sometimes,
that's the best lead you can have. Let's focus
on Tom Hampton next."

Perry Light Rail Station
West Colfax Neighborhood
West Denver
8:25 p.m.

Twenty-two year old Mariel Reyna
stepped out onto the platform at Sperry
Station and into a beautiful night. Despite
knowing it was too soon to declare spring

had arrived, she reveled in the euphoria of surviving another long Colorado winter.

Walking down the station steps, she crossed a patch of grass to a tiny, wood fence—more of a decoration than a barrier—and hopped it. Her parents' home was located on South Quitman Street, a dead end next to the rail station, and her walk to the house took less than two minutes.

A light breeze tussled her shoulder-length auburn hair but did not produce sufficient chill to require the red jacket she carried over her arm. She found herself humming as she walked. The house was hers for the night, with her parents being out of town, and she planned on enjoying the solitude.

She loved her folks, but she longed to have her own space. Nevertheless, moving out would have to wait until Miguel got out of the service. They planned to get married then get a place of their own. In the meantime, whenever her folks were gone, she treasured the peaceful evenings.

She smiled to herself, remembering his face when he'd pointed at her, then at his chest, and then announced their nickname—M&M.

"I'm a peanut and you're a smooth chocolate."

Then he would laugh and declare that one day they would have a house full of M&M'S.

As she headed up the driveway, she noticed an unfamiliar car sitting across the street, the parking lights on. A man appeared to be watching her, but because of the darkness, his face was hidden. Her senses heightened, she quickened her pace and had her key ready when she got to the door. Without looking back, she let herself in then slammed the door behind her.

Only after the slide bolt was in place did she peel back the curtain enough to peek outside.

The car was gone.

She scanned for a moment longer then sighed.

You're being paranoid, Mariel.

She decided the absence of her parents and the death of Carole Hampton was making her jumpy.

Chiding herself for being afraid, she laid down her stuff and went into the kitchen. Leftover enchiladas would make for a yummy dinner. She retrieved them from the fridge and stuck them in the microwave before going upstairs.

Dressed in pajamas when she returned downstairs, she inhaled deeply, and the aroma of the reheated food filled her senses and drew a rumble from her stomach. The enchiladas allowed her to push the stranger to the back of her mind.

Elway's Steakhouse & Lounge Cherry Creek Shopping Center Southeast Denver 8:45 p.m.

Like Michael Jordan in Chicago, Wayne Gretzky in Edmonton, and Mickey Mantle in New York, John Elway was a name synonymous with the Mile-High City. As a result, his four namesake steakhouses were rated among the best in Denver, as well as being among the most expensive.

Although the place was more than a little pricey for a detective's pay scale, Tanner and Laura nevertheless enjoyed the atmosphere. On top of that, they both loved the Truffled Fries, one of the few things they could afford. When Kate had decided to call it a night, Tanner had phoned Laura and arranged their date.

Polished mahogany, plush chairs and subdued lighting surrounded them as they finished up their treat. He still wondered how he got so lucky. Laura, her jet-black hair hanging on a white, button-front blouse and her green eyes reflecting the lights in the room, was a vision to the tired detective.

"You look gorgeous."

She smiled. "Thank you very much. You, on the other hand, look worn out."

He laughed. "Thank you very much. You're so kind to notice."

"Think nothing of it. Everything okay at work?"

His smile faded. "Fine, at least the work part of it."

"What other part is there?"

"Well, I learned something from Kate that has me unsettled."

"Oh? Such as?"

"Well, you can't say anything."

She looked over both shoulders then back at him. "To who? I don't know any of your cop friends."

"Fair enough. Kate has put in for a transfer out of Homicide."

Laura was obviously unmoved by the gravity of this news. "Okay…"

"It's a big deal."

"Why?"

"Because she's the best. She's one of
the most successful and admired detectives
in the department's history. Her solve rate is
well over ninety percent, even though she's
given the most difficult cases."

"So, you'll be losing a good detective.
She's eventually going to retire, anyway."

Tanner sipped his beer. "I know,
but…"

Laura's eyes widened. "Wait—is she
leaving because of you?"

Tanner laughed. "That was my first
thought! Not according to her."

"Then why?"

"She said she doesn't want a long line
of dead bodies to be her only memories of
the job."

Laura sipped her drink, a strawberry
margarita. Her eyes were locked with his. "I
guess I can understand that."

Tanner shrugged. "Me, too. But there's
more to it than that. She's as tough as they
come, and if the job can get to her, what will
it do to me?"

A silence fell between them, and
Tanner sensed Laura was weighing his
question with equal concern. After all, soon
it wouldn't be just his life, but theirs.

The question remained unanswered by
either of them.

<u>Wednesday, April 8</u>

South Quitman Street
West Colfax Neighborhood
West Denver
12:25 a.m.

He pulled an armchair forward, positioning it at just the right angle for his work. Tucking the gun in his belt loop, he went about the business of pulling out his tools. A rough-surface drawing pad, a small blending stick, and several Conté crayons—all black. He was uninterested in color, be it furniture or clothing.

He studied his subject for several minutes as he prepared to draw. The one lamp he'd left on in the living room cast a perfect compromise of shadow and illumination for his purpose. Her shirt and bra lay on the floor next to the bright-red couch, on which he'd posed her for the portrait.

He'd placed her head at an angle that pleased him, her shoulder-length brown hair swept to one side and forward, which provided an elegant flair and contrast to her soft features. He'd removed her clothing to give the drawing a sense of naked emotion, much as it would have been when she was born.

Like most, she had co-operated, moving as he instructed, but her eyes betrayed the fear, even as she fought to maintain the calm he demanded. His words and his low tone of voice were an effort to soothe her. His desire was not to have panic reflected in the picture, but peace, as if his subject was there voluntarily.

"We should be done in an hour or so, and then I'll leave. If you maintain the position I request, it will speed things up."

He gave the same encouragement to all his subjects, trying to eliminate tears, which resulted in swelling of the face. They always seemed to believe him, or maybe it was just blind hope registering in their eyes.

Satisfied, he began to draw. Hesitantly, at first, then faster.

His art was about chronicling the time just before the death of his subject, capturing forever the final moments of a life. Few things in art could equal the emotion and insight his drawings held.

His hand moved steadily across the Strathmore 400 drawing pad, laying down the outline of his subject. Her form took shape quickly, the flow of his hand unchecked by any hint of uncertainty, his eye practiced at transferring the vision before him to the artist's pad.

The silence in the room, with exception of the sound of her shallow, nervous breathing, was perfect for him to concentrate and produce his work. He reveled in the image appearing before him, his excitement flowing from the knowledge of what the work represented, and the final act that drew ever closer as the portrait neared completion.

His focus intensified, as he began to apply the finer details to the sketch. He was meticulous in making sure the length and flow of her hair was just right. Her nose, the curve of her mouth, the thickness of her eyebrows, the shape of her eyes; these all had to be precise.

It wasn't just about making a transcendent piece of art, but the responsibility he felt to capture his subject's final minutes accurately.

Without warning, her body convulsed in a choking cough, breaking his concentration. She covered her mouth, fear widening her eyes. Her change of position, especially at such a critical moment in the process, was unacceptable. As he glared at her, she did her best to resume the pose.

He scowled at her effort.

"Lift your chin."

She did.

"Turn your body more to the side."

Awkwardly, she attempted to do so without moving her head; she failed.

Setting down his pad, he crossed the room, stopping close enough to tower over her. Instinctively, she shrank from him, further distorting the pose he sought.

"Stop moving! I'll show you again, but don't make me do this a third time. Is that clear?"

She nodded, her eyes welling up.

"And don't cry!"

Somehow, she didn't.

Returning to his chair after readjusting his subject, he studied his sketch then her new position, then the sketch again; finally, he decided he could continue. His hands resumed their methodical drawing, but the surge of adrenaline had taken away some of his precision.

He paused, closed his eyes, and took in a deep breath.

After letting it out slowly, he repeated the process two more times.

When he opened his eyes after the third time and restarted drawing, his gracefulness had returned. After several minutes, the picture was nearing completion and just needed the finishing touches. When he took a final glance at his subject, she was crying.

The crayon snapped in his hand as rage took over.

"What is wrong with you, girl? Do you want me to have to start a new drawing? You're ruining the work at its most crucial point!"

She wiped at her eyes. "I'm sorry."

Seething, he studied his work, deciding he had no choice but to let it suffice—though it wasn't to the artistic level he was accustomed to achieving.

From his art bag, he retrieved a can of spray fixative and lightly coated the drawing. It would seal the sketch from smudging.

After carefully retrieving his broken Conté, he put everything back into the art satchel, stood, and approached his subject. His soothing tone returned.

"Okay, it's over. You can relax now. Take that pillow, lie back against the couch, and cover your face."

She seemed incapable of unlocking her body from her pose but stole a glance at the throw pillow. "Why?"

"I'm getting ready to leave. I want you to cover your face and count to one hundred."

Uncertainty showed clearly on her face, but probably because the pillow offered some covering for her exposed body, she relented. He handed her the pillow.

"That's perfect. Just start counting, and don't stop until you reach one hundred. I'll be gone when you finish."

The muffled sound of her hopeful counting came through the pillow.

"One, two, three…"

He listened as she passed ten, then twenty, and finally thirty.

Basking in the power he held at that moment—the complete control over his art, a life, and a death—he experienced fully the emotion that fueled his passion to create.

Before her counting reached forty, he pulled out his gun, pressed it to the pillow, and fired twice.

JOHN C. DALGLISH

Denver Art Museum
Civic Center Park
West 14th Avenue Parkway
Downtown Denver
9:20 a.m.

Situated in the heart of the city, the Denver Art Museum—the DAM to the locals—could also lay claim to being the cultural heartbeat of the West. One of the largest museums between the Pacific Ocean and Chicago, it was considered a must-see for residents and visitors alike who came to the Mile-High City.

Works by famous artists, familiar to even the most novice enthusiasts—names such as Matisse, Picasso, and Monet—were found in the expansive halls of the DAM. However, its biggest contribution might have been the expansive collection of Native American art, acquired and promoted since 1925.

While the museum's street address put it on Fourteenth Avenue, across from the Greek Amphitheater at Civic Park, the rambling collection of structures extended all the way down to Twelfth Avenue. A covered pedestrian bridge over Thirteenth Avenue connected the display halls to each other.

Something of this magnitude took a lot of people to run, most of whom the average visitor would never meet. One of the staff that a patron was likely to interact with was a docent. The faces of the museum, docents gave tours to groups, individuals, and school classes. They were very good at telling stories and bringing the exhibits to life.

In the life of Paul Ridley, they were critical.

As the Museum Educator, he oversaw the docent staff and scheduled tours, which explained, in part, why this day had gotten off to such a poor start. His most trusted volunteer, who happened to also be his best tour guide, was late.

"Has anyone heard from Mariel?"

The Welcome Center staff responded to his inquiry with blank stares.

Ridley rubbed his hands together worriedly. An entire busload of fourth graders was due any minute, and Mariel was supposed to be their guide.

Another staff member came into the office. He searched her face hopefully.

"Joanna! Have you heard from Mariel?"

The Public Relations Officer stopped and looked at him. "Mariel Reyna?"

"Yeah. Have you seen her?"

Joanna shook her long chestnut-brown hair and adjusted her black, wide-framed glasses on her delicate nose. "Nope. Sorry."

Through the welcome center window, Paul spotted the school bus coming to a stop. Without Mariel, he was the only one who could fill-in, and he *really* didn't have the time. But neither did he have a choice.

"Okay, if Mariel shows up, tell her I'm taking the tour and starting in the Hamilton building."

There were nods all around.

He turned and headed out to meet the kids, but in the back of his mind, he fretted. Mariel was the epitome of reliability; she had never missed a day without calling.

I hope she didn't get in a wreck.

The screeching coming from the kids piling off the bus pushed his concerns into the background.

Residence of Mr. & Mrs. Reyna
South Quitman Street
West Colfax Neighborhood
West Denver
10:00 a.m.

The yellow Crown Victoria stopped at the curb of their home, and the driver popped the trunk release. Mr. Reyna waited for his wife to get out then met the driver at the back of the car. Handing over the fare, he took possession of their two bags and thanked the cabbie.

"Have a good day."

"Thank you, sir. You and your wife do the same."

The cab was already gone by the time Reyna reached his wife, who was about to insert her key into the door when it glided open. She looked back at him, concern racing across her face. He met her eyes briefly then pushed past her.

"Wait here."

He left the bags on the stoop with his wife and moved into the front foyer.

"Mariel?"

Greeted by silence, he called louder.

"Mariel!"

His wife started to follow him inside, and he pointed at the front yard.

"Stay outside until I know it's safe."

"She's my daughter, too. I'll not wait for you to wander around the house." She started up the steps. "Mariel, are you here?"

He let her go, moving into the living room. Something was out of place, but his mind couldn't pinpoint it immediately. When it did, he grew agitated. For some reason, Mariel had dragged an armchair into the middle of the room.

Mr. Reyna started to move it back to its proper place when a coppery odor stopped him.

He had been in war; he knew the smell of blood.

His gaze quickly settled on the throw pillow and the blood congealing below it.

"Nooooo!"

Denver Police Department
District 2 Precinct
Holly Street
10:20 a.m.

Kate and Tanner were going over their case files when the lieutenant leaned out of his office.

111

"Detective Walker!"

"Sir?"

"My office, pronto."

She stood. "Austin, as well?"

"Just you."

He disappeared back into his office, and Kate turned to Tanner.

"I wonder what he's all worked up about."

"You go find out. Me? I'm gonna stay right here."

She rolled her eyes. "Thanks for the support."

He laughed. "Hey, I got your back—just from out here."

She ignored him and made her way to the lieutenant's office, leaning through the door.

"What's up?"

He gestured toward a chair.

"Close the door, and pull up a seat."

She did. When she was seated, and staring at him, she realized Frank was upset, not angry.

"What is it, Frank?"

Without a word, he laid a sheet of paper on the desk between them. She immediately recognized her transfer request.

"Oh, that. I see you got it."

"Brilliant deduction. You should be a detective—or should I say *stay* a detective."

She allowed a smile, but he didn't return it.

The paper remained where he put it, neither of them wanting to touch it, as if doing so would cross some invisible line.

He sighed. "Let me start by saying how shocked I was to get this."

"I understand."

"Do you? Because I'm not sure you do."

"What do you mean?"

He folded his arms across his ample stomach and leaned back. "Perhaps an example would help. In your opinion, who's the greatest guitar player of all time?"

She raised a single eyebrow. "What?"

"Humor me. Who do you think was the greatest guitar player of all time?"

She shrugged. "Jimi Hendrix?"

"Okay, and let's say you are Mr. Hendrix's manager and friend."

"Okaaaay."

"And one night, Jimi calls you and says he has some news. So, you say, 'what's up, Jimi?' To which he responds, 'I've decided to give up the guitar; I'm never gonna play again. Instead, I'm trying to learn the flute.'"

Kate stared at him, doing her best to follow his train of thought without laughing.

"The flute?"

113

Frank nodded. "Yeah. The flute."

"Okay, the flute."

"What would you say to Jimi?"

She didn't even have to think about it, which she realized was the point.

"I'd say, 'are you crazy?'"

Frank leaned forward. "Makes sense. What else?"

"Oh, probably something like—you're one of the best, ever; why give it up?"

Frank was nodding. "Sure, and what else?"

"I don't know. Maybe... you have a tremendous gift; why waste it?"

"Exactly!"

Her lieutenant slammed a meaty hand down on the desk so hard, she jerked in her chair. His face had taken on a shade of red she hadn't seen before.

"So, now I'm asking you all the same questions! Are you crazy? You're one of the best, ever; why give it up? You're a gifted investigator; why waste such talent?"

He stared at her, a heavy silence filling the space between them. Not usually at a loss for words, she found herself unable to form a defense.

The color slowly drained from Frank's face, returning his skin tone to a semblance of normal. He sighed. "Look, I know that's kinda dramatic, but I don't get it. Public relations?"

She leaned back and sucked in a long breath.

"Look, Frank, I see what you're doing, and I appreciate it. Really."

His tone had turned softer. "But?"

"I've given this job everything, literally. I don't have much of a personal life, some might argue none, and I'm not sure what I'm going to do when I retire."

Frank nodded but didn't interrupt.

"So, I got to thinking about my career and the memories I would have, and you know what I came up with?"

"What?"

"Bodies."

"I'm sorry?"

"Bodies, corpses, Frank. A long line of murdered, mutilated, devastated people from each of the cases I've worked since coming to Homicide. That's what I envision looking back on when I retire."

She paused, expecting to see a level of surprise from her outburst. Instead, his face reflected understanding.

"Me, too."

For a moment, she thought she'd heard wrong. "What?"

"Me, too. I worry about being woke up in the night, visions of past cases robbing me of my sleep. In fact, I considered leaving Homicide myself a while back."

Kate suspected her jaw of hitting the desk. "Really? It never occurred to me... But you didn't?"

"Nope."

"Why not?"

"I had a friend who was a detective in Boulder. I told him what I was thinking, and he invited me down for a visit. So I went."

He paused, seemingly traveling back there in his mind.

"My buddy knew I loved Shakespeare, so he got us tickets to the Colorado Shakespeare Festival. It was fabulous, especially in the giant, outdoor amphitheater they have, and it lifted my spirits."

"So you think I need to see a play?"

Frank smiled. "No, but afterward, we went out to dinner. During the meal, he asked me who I thought the greatest playwright was."

"Let me guess—Shakespeare?"

"That's right. Then he asked me the same question I asked you. What if William Shakespeare had told me he wanted to quit writing?"

Kate smiled. "And you answered the same way."

"I did."

116

"But that doesn't change the way I feel about my future."

"No, and it didn't change my mind, either."

"So what did?"

"My friend gave me one thing to think about before letting me make a final decision."

Kate stared, sensing in herself a little hope. Maybe a different outcome to the future she saw was possible.

Frank leaned in close. "My friend said this: 'We are all given a talent, and if we use it, we'll leave an impact on the world we lived in. If we turn our back on that gift, we will never reach the degree of satisfaction we were intended to have.'"

Kate absorbed the words, seeking life in them.

Frank leaned back and fixed her with a poignant gaze. "Kate, when you look back on your life, it won't be bodies you see, but those who remained alive. The ones you helped make whole again."

She began to see the wisdom in his words but still felt the weight of all she'd seen in her career.

The phone began to buzz, interrupting any further discussion. Frank picked it up.

"Yeah?"

He listened for a moment, then made a couple notes on the pad in front of him. His gaze flipped up to Kate, and she transferred her focus from their conversation to the one Frank was having on the phone.

When he hung up, he handed her a slip of paper. "You've got a scene. The responding officer suggested to the dispatcher that it might be tied to your Hampton case."

Kate stood, accepting the paper. "Did they say who the officer was?"

"Pope."

The name was familiar. She started to leave but hesitated. "Frank... I appreciate...thanks."

"You're welcome."

She turned and opened the door to go.

"Oh, Kate."

She turned back. "Yeah."

He was holding up the transfer notice. "Do you want this?"

She stared at it for a long moment. "Not sure. I'll let you know."

"Fair enough."

Residence of Mr. & Mrs. Reyna
South Quitman Street
West Colfax Neighborhood
West Denver
11:30 a.m.

On the way to the scene, Tanner refreshed Kate's memory on who the officer was that recommended them.

"Pope is the one who called a couple days later with the tip on Blackwell."

She nodded as they pulled up at the scene. "Of course. Well, he saw something here that set off alarm bells."

Tanner turned off the car. "Let's hope he's wrong."

"My sentiments, exactly."

They climbed out into the warm sun, and if they weren't about to walk into a murder scene, Tanner's spirit would have been buoyed by the warmth. A light breeze rocked the crime scene tape back and forth gently.

Tanner cast a glance toward the front door of the modest-looking, two-story home. White siding and redbrick fascia seemed to clash, but the yard was nicely landscaped.

The first perennial flowers were just now beginning to show. He guessed the scene inside would be considerably less idyllic.

They approached the perimeter, holding out their badges to the officer on duty.

The officer lifted the tape. "Hey, Detectives."

Kate tucked away her badge. "Officer Pope still here?"

"Yeah. I believe he's inside with the parents."

Tanner's stomach tightened. *Parents. That means our victim is likely a child.*

Kate glanced back at him as he came under the tape. They exchanged looks, and he recognized the same uneasiness in her eyes.

Every detective dreaded being called out on a child's murder, but no case made a detective work harder and longer to catch a killer than one involving a juvenile.

As they got to the front door, Officer Pope came out.

"Detective Austin, Detective Walker. Thanks for coming."

Tanner shook Pope's hand. "Of course. What have you got?"

Pope pulled out his notepad.

"Female, twenty-two, dead from apparent gunshot. Her name is Mariel

Reyna, and she was found this morning by her parents."

Kate looked down the road. "Coroner in route?"

"Yes, ma'am."

"Have you touched anything?"

"No."

Tanner looked through the door but couldn't see the body. "Why did you suspect she was tied to the Hampton killing?"

Pope put away his notebook. Apparently, he didn't need notes to remember what he'd seen.

"She was topless, lying back on a couch, a pillow over her face. There are two holes in the pillow."

Tanner sighed. "Sounds like the same method used on Carole Hampton."

Kate started inside. "Good call, Pope."

"Thank you, ma'am."

While his partner went inside, Tanner asked about the discovery.

"So you say the parents found her?"

"That's right. They had been out of town and found the door unlocked when they arrived home. The father discovered his daughter in the living room."

"Where are they now?"

"In the kitchen."

"Good. Start a neighborhood canvas for us, okay?"

"I'll get right on it."

Tanner went inside. The home was decorated much like the exterior. Modest but tidy. To the left of the entrance, he found the living room, as well as Kate. She appeared to be studying the body.

"Was Pope right?"

She nodded. "Looks like it, but I don't want to move the pillow until after photos are taken. See that?"

Tanner followed her gesture toward the end of the room. Sitting ajar, obviously out of place, was an armchair.

"Just like the make-up bench at the Hampton scene, huh?"

"A little too odd, don't you think?"

Tanner moved over by the chair and kneeled down. "Yeah, but what is it for?"

"He could be watching them or taunting them. Who knows what else!"

The carpet was a low-pile variety, but he could still make out the impression of a bag. "Kate, look."

She kneeled beside him. "Looks the same. We need good photos of it."

At that moment, the crime scene processing team arrived. Kate stood and met with the main tech.

Tanner was studying the impression when his gaze was drawn to something else—black shards or crumbs—scattered under the chair.

"Hey, have you got some tape?"

The tech talking to Kate nodded.

"Sure. Why?"

"Bring me a piece, and a bag."

The female tech and Kate came over to where he was kneeling. Kate produced an evidence bag while the tech handed Tanner some clear masking tape. He peeled a large piece off the roll and folded it back on itself.

With the sticky side out, he dabbed at the tiny black particles, getting all of them to adhere to the tape. He then took another piece of tape and sealed the particles, so they wouldn't be lost. Finally, he inserted his little package into the bag Kate was holding.

She sealed the bag and held it up to look at it. "I don't remember seeing those at the Hampton scene, do you?"

Tanner stood. "Nope."

The tech took the bag and went back outside, presumably to secure the evidence. Kate took out her recorder and began her normal ritual.

"Victim is lying back on couch, has pants on, but is naked above the waist. Blouse and bra are on floor next to victim. Only one lamp is on in the room, and nothing has been disturbed other than one chair. Chair is located as if to observe the victim…"

Her hesitation prompted Tanner to look at her, but she ignored him and continued.

"Throw pillow is covering face and upper torso, two holes are present in the pillow, and evidence of gunpowder stippling is…" She clicked off the recorder. "Where are the parents?"

"Pope said they were in the kitchen."

Tanner stared at her as she headed for the kitchen and didn't think to follow her until she was already out of the room. When he did catch up with her, she was sitting at a wooden kitchen table, her faced fixed in a blank expression.

He'd not seen her act this way before.

Tanner stopped by the door and leaned against the frame. Mr. and Mrs. Reyna seemed to be shrinking before his eyes. Both were small in stature, anyway, but they appeared to be sliding beneath the dining table, as if trying to hide from the truth that was now their life.

The silver-haired couple held hands, and while Mrs. Reyna repeatedly used her other hand to dab at her eyes, Mr. Reyna let his tears flow. Tanner listened quietly to the couple as they tried to answer Kate's questions.

She didn't have her pad out, and though her questions were direct, they were tinged with sympathy.

"Does your daughter work?"

"Yes. She works downtown at the Art Museum."

"Does she have any connection to DIA?"

"The airport? Not that I know of. She's flown out of there before, of course."

Kate nodded "Of course. Does she take any classes at Colorado College of Art?"

"No."

"Has she ever?"

"Taken classes there?"

Kate nodded.

Mr. Reyna seemed to think for a minute. "Not that I can remember."

"What about enemies? Had your daughter indicated if she was afraid of someone?"

Reyna looked at his wife, who shook her head weakly. He agreed. "She got along with everyone."

"Did she have a boyfriend?"

"She's engaged to a soldier, but he's overseas right now."

Kate's questions were coming quickly, perhaps too quickly for the elderly couple.

"Does your daughter own a car?"

"A car...no. She takes the RTD."

Tanner's adrenaline spiked. Trains had cameras, and RTD trains produced high-definition video. He and Kate exchanged glances, and he guessed she was on the same page as he was.

She continued. "So, where would she get off when she was headed home?"

Mr. Reyna tipped his head toward the north.

"The Sperry station at the end of our street."

"When was the last time you spoke with your daughter?"

This question set Mrs. Reyna to sobbing. Kate reached across the table to touch the woman's arm.

"I'm so sorry."

Mr. Reyna was barely holding it together himself. "We spoke to her the morning we left. That was the last..."

The unfinished sentence broke Mr. Reyna.

Together, the parents let out their pain.

Tanner's heart ached as he watched them. He hadn't known the name Mariel Reyna this morning, but like all the cases he'd worked, he would never forget it now.

Kate stood. "Mr. Reyna, I know how difficult this is, but you'll need to go downtown with one of our officers and give a full statement."

Mr. Reyna nodded.

Kate turned and headed out of the kitchen, suddenly appearing irritated.

Tagging along behind her, Tanner caught up with her outside. He paused next to her, as she stood on the front lawn, gazing toward the north end of the cul-de-sac.

"Did the Reynas do something wrong?"

She shook her head. "No, of course not."

"Then why do I sense you're pissed?"

She avoided looking at him. "Later. Right now, we need video from that rail station. Our victim may have been followed from the train."

Tanner nodded. "I'll see if the parents can pinpoint the time she may have gotten home, then I'll make a call to RTD headquarters."

Kate turned back to him. "What's taking that freakin' coroner so long?"

Unsure what the holdup was, Tanner was glad about one thing.

He wasn't the one who had to explain it to Kate.

The Delectable Egg
1642 Market Street
Downtown
12:45 p.m.

Tanner had secured an appointment to look at Regional Transportation's security tape, but the comptroller wouldn't be available until two o'clock. Since the RTD offices just happened to be a block over from Kate's favorite restaurant and they hadn't eaten, she had proposed they get some lunch.

Tanner had pulled the car into the RTD lot, and then he and Kate had walked through the warm afternoon to the bistro. During the meal, Kate had remained quiet, still angry about the reality she'd been faced with while speaking to Mariel Reyna's parents. Now, on the way back to the RTD offices, Tanner's unease about her mood was obvious.

"What is it, Austin?"

He cast a tentative smile her way. "What is what?"

"Reading people is what we do, remember? Out with it."

"Fair enough."

They were crossing a public greenspace between Market and Blake Streets, and when she spotted an empty bench, she sat down. Tanner sat next to her. "So, I don't get it. Why get so aggravated at the Reynas'? They had just lost their only daughter."

As they stared out at the passersby, she weighed her answer. Finally, she sighed.

"Think about it, Tanner. Tom Hampton almost certainly is not connected to our second victim. Blackwell, while in the art field, never had her as a student. We would have to come up with more to claim a direct connection between them. Therefore, we're probably back to square one."

"Sure, but that happens, right?"

"Of course, but that's not what jerks my chain."

"Okay, I'll bite. What does?"

"We spent the last two-plus days investigating nothing. While we were off chasing ghosts, this animal was planning and then carrying out another murder."

Tanner was slow to grasp her direction. "We did what we could with what we had."

"Did we?"

"I don't follow."

Another deep breath and sigh. "Don't you wonder what we missed? Aren't you asking yourself what we didn't see that allowed us to waste the last two days?"

Tanner didn't have an answer, and she found her own words were draining the anger out of her. Instead, a feeling of despair was taking its place.

She stood up. "I can't help it. I wonder if Mariel Reyna would still be alive if we'd done our job better."

Tanner looked up at her. "You can't do that, Kate. It'll kill you."

A sad smile crossed her lips. "Now you have some idea of why I put in for a transfer."

She turned and headed for the RTD offices, and only after nearly a minute of walking, realized he hadn't followed her. When she turned around, he was still on the bench, staring at the sky. She walked back.

"Hey, it's almost two o'clock."

He pushed himself to his feet. "You're wrong."

"I'm sorry?"

His facial muscles were taut as his emotions churned to the surface. "We *didn't* waste our time, and we couldn't have stopped another killing. The truth is—if it hadn't been Mariel, it would have been another girl."

"Why do you say that?"

"What are you always telling me?"

She grinned. "That's a long list."

He ignored the humor. "Read the scene. You're always saying the crime scene will tell a story, right?"

"That's right."

"Well, what was the story at the Hampton scene?"

His eyes fixed on hers, but he didn't wait for an answer.

"To me, it said Carole Hampton was not his first victim or even his second. This guy is practiced, he's smart, and he's careful. Killers like him don't get caught until they make a mistake, which they rarely do, and my gut says he didn't make that mistake at the Hampton scene."

His voice cracked with conviction, the passion of his belief flowing from every word. He was staring hard at her now, pushing as an equal. "Our job is to find his mistake, and then stop another killing from ever happening."

She had come to the same conclusion as he had when it came to the scenes. She met his stare.

"So, it's about saving the next victim?"

He nodded. "With a serial killer, it's always about the next victim—for him and for us."

She studied him, finding a depth to him that she didn't remember seeing or perhaps just hadn't noticed before. Despite the warmth of the sun, a chill ran through her.

What else have I missed lately?

Is it possible I've become too embroiled in my own issues?

What if I miss something—not because it isn't there, but because I've lost focus?

The idea sickened her. "We need to send out our guy's M.O., and see if anyone has a similar case."

Tanner nodded. "When we get back to the station, I'll send it out to the whole state."

"Good. Now, are we going to stop this guy?"

Appearing relieved, he smiled. "Dang straight!"

She glanced down at her watch. "Then I suppose we shouldn't be late for our appointment."

Regional Transportation District Headquarters
1600 Blake Street
Downtown
2:00 p.m.

The RTD Headquarters was a squat, sprawling, four-story structure made of brick. The arches over each window gave it an older look than it deserved, especially since the interior was full of modern technology. The comptroller was sitting behind a large, wooden desk, waiting for them in his fourth-floor office.

"Come in, Detectives." He nodded at Tanner. "I'm David."

Tanner showed his badge. "I'm Detective Austin."

David dismissed the formality with a wave. "No need, Detective. I've known Kate for years."

Tanner realized his partner and the comptroller were smiling at each other. Kate took a seat in front of the desk.

"How have you been David?"

"Good."

"How are the girls?"

"Great. They ask about you often."

"Tell them I said hi."

"I will. You should come over sometime and have dinner with us."

Tanner looked at his partner, her gentle side revealing itself so suddenly, he was staring. David cleared his throat and offered a seat to Tanner, who accepted.

Picking up a remote, David aimed it at a large monitor on the wall. "So, I pulled the film from around the time you gave me. This is inside the *W* train as it moves from Knox Station to Sperry. Tell me if you see your girl."

The pictures slowly cycled through the interior of several train cars, pausing for them to inspect the riders. Finally, when they reached the fourth car, both Tanner and Kate sat forward.

"There!" they said in unison.

Sitting by herself was Mariel Reyna, the other people on her car seemingly uninterested in the young woman. Tanner pointed at each person while counting.

"One, two, three, four women. One man."

The video moved forward, and they watched as the train slowed then stopped. Mariel stood and exited the train. No one from her car followed her.

David paused the playback. "This is Sperry Station. I'll pick it up from the platform camera."

The picture changed to show the length of the station, and as it moved forward, numerous individuals entered and exited the cars. Mariel came off her car and walked toward the east end of the platform, which happened to be the opposite direction of everyone else.

No one spoke to her, and she went down the steps alone. The train pulled away, and in moments, they were looking at an empty platform.

Kate shook her head. "I don't see anything unusual."

Tanner slumped back in his chair. "She wasn't followed, at least not from the station."

Kate wanted another look. "Play it one more time, David?"

"Sure."

The video ran again, a little slower this time, from the moment Mariel got off the train car. The result was the same. Nobody even looked her way.

Kate sighed. "That's disappointing. Can we get a copy anyway, David?"

"Of course. I'll have it sent over to the precinct."

Kate stood. "Good to see you again."

David came around his desk and stood in front of her. "Same here. Come by when you can stay longer."

She laughed. "You know how it is. Always seems like life is too busy."

David smiled, and Tanner sensed a reluctance on the man's part to let Kate leave. Eventually, she turned and headed for the door.

Tanner caught up with her in the hallway. "You two go way back, I guess?"

"Yeah. I met him around the time he lost his wife. He's good people."

"What happened?"

She shook her head. "I'll tell you some other time. Let's focus on the job at hand, okay?"

"Fair enough. Have you got an idea where we should go next?"

"We need to find or remove the connections between victims one and two."

"Tom Hampton?"

"Tom Hampton."

Hampton Residence
Montbello Neighborhood
Northeast Denver
3:15 p.m.

Tom Hampton greeted them at the door. Despite being out of the hospital, his appearance hadn't improved much. His face was drawn and tired, several days' of growth covered his chin, and his clothes were wrinkled.

"Come in, Detectives."

Kate tried a weak smile. "Thanks, Mr. Hampton."

"Tom, please."

Tanner followed Kate in, closing the door behind him. The rooms were dark, and after leading them into the living room, Tom turned on a lamp.

"You want to sit down?"

Kate declined. "Thanks, no. We don't want to take up too much of your time."

"Suit yourself." Tom dropped into an overstuffed armchair, a half-empty glass of a dark liquid on the table next to him.

"Ice tea?" he asked, lifting his glass. "It's in the fridge."

Kate was relieved to discover the dark liquid was tea. "No, thanks."

Tanner also declined.

Tom took a sip. "Tomorrow's the day."

Kate raised an eyebrow. "The day?"

"Carole's funeral. The coroner released her body."

"When is it?"

"Two o'clock. She's being buried next to her mom in Riverside."

"That's a beautiful place."

He set the glass back on the table. "So, is there any news?"

"Of a sort. Tom, does the name Mariel Reyna mean anything to you?"

"Reyna?" Tom rubbed his chin. "No. Can't say I've ever heard it before. Why?"

"She was found dead, and we believe the same person who killed Carole may be responsible."

Tom blanched. "Another dead woman?"

"I'm afraid so."

"When?"

"We believe she was killed late last night or early this morning."

Tom leaned forward, looking as if he might vomit. "Ungodly animal, whoever he is."

Kate took a quick glance at Tanner, who was taking notes. His faced reflected the sadness they were all feeling. She turned back to Tom, dreading her next question.

"I know this is lousy, but I have to ask."

Tom nodded. "Whatever you need."

"Where were you last night?"

Whatever he expected her to ask, clearly, that hadn't been it. He looked up at her, his hands dropping to his sides. "Seriously?"

"I'm afraid so. It's just a formality, I assure you."

"Unbelievable." He shook his head slowly. "You think I could kill my wife, then move on to a total stranger?"

Kate forced herself not to get defensive. "We're not trying to suggest that, but we have a job to do."

Tom's tone turned defiant. "I was here! My son was with me all night and slept on the couch."

"Where is your son now?"

"He's at the funeral home, finishing up my wife's arrangements. You can wait for him if you want."

Kate shook her head. "That won't be necessary. Our other victim worked at the Denver Art Museum. Did Carole have any connection with the DAM?"

"Sure. She was on the community advisory board."

Kate's attention intensified. "Advisory board?"

"Yeah. It's a link between the museum's leadership and the community.

Carole volunteered for it after she left the airline."

"Do you know who heads the board?"

"A guy named Palmer, I think."

Kate checked with Tanner to make sure he was getting it all down. When he nodded, she stood. "Thank you, Mr. Hampton. We'll see ourselves out."

"Uh… Detective."

"Yes."

"Give my sympathies to the Reyna family."

"Yes, sir. I'll do that."

They were back in the car and headed toward the precinct when Kate's phone buzzed in her pocket. "Detective Walker."

"Kate, it's Dana."

"Hi, Doc. What have you got?"

"I'm about to do the autopsy on the Reyna girl. Just wanted you to know."

Kate stole a glance at the time. "We were just headed to the precinct. We'll come there instead. Thanks, Doc."

She hung up.

"Dana McCloud is starting the autopsy on Mariel Reyna. We'll miss the show, but we can catch the report."

"Sounds good. As for Tom Hampton, do we cross him off?"

"I think so. Especially if his alibi checks out, which I assume it will."

"Me, too."

She cast a sideways glance at her young partner. "We should go."

"Go?"

"To the funeral."

He nodded. "See who attends?"

"Yeah. And pay our respects."

"Count me in."

Office of the Medical Examiner
686 Bannock Street
Lincoln Park District
5:10 p.m.

They checked the observatory and discovered they were too late. The autopsy was over, so their next stop was Dana's office. Tanner knocked on the office doorframe. "Hey?"

Dana looked up. "Hey, yourself."

Kate pulled up a seat at the desk. Dana held up a finger.

"One sec. Just finishing the rough draft."

After a couple moments, Dana sat back, her face the image of a long day. Tanner was unaccustomed to seeing the coroner look so tired.

"Rough day, Doc?"

"Long and taxing, both mentally and physically—but enough about me."

She smiled briefly then picked up a folder. "Mariel Reyna was killed by two shots to the forehead, same as Carole Hampton. The caliber matches, both being twenty-fives. Both slugs were in decent shape this time, and they've been sent to ballistics for matching to the Walker slug."

Tanner had his pad out. "Sexual assault?"

"No."

"What about TOD?"

"Sometime between Midnight and three in the morning."

"Did you find any trace evidence?"

Dana shook her head. "This guy, whoever he is, was careful. Nothing on the body or under the fingernails."

Tanner closed his pad. "What about the particles we found on the floor?"

"You'll have to check with the lab on those. Otherwise, that's all I've got."

Kate stood. "Thanks, Dana. Forward the report to us?"

"As always. Good luck."

Walking back out to the car, Tanner called the Forensic Lab.

"Denver Forensic Lab. This is Zimmer."

"This is Detective Austin. I'm calling about some samples from the Reyna case."

"The black particles?"

"Yeah. Do you have any results?"

"Just the basic analysis. They appear to be from some sort of crayon, but we can't identify them exactly. We've sent the samples off to the Colorado Bureau lab in Arvada."

"Any idea how long?"

"A couple days to a week. Hard to say for sure."

"Okay, thanks."

Tanner hung up to find Kate watching him. "What's the hold up?"

"Our guys identified the particles as a kind of crayon, but they can't pinpoint the origin exactly. They sent them over to the new CBI lab."

"How long?"

"Too long."

DENVER HOMICIDE

<u>Thursday, April 9</u>

*Denver Police Department
District 2 Precinct
Holly Street
8:20 a.m.*

Tanner had faxed out their case description before going home the previous night. The first thing he did when he arrived was check the machine for responses. Optimism born of a new day was quickly dashed when he realized there was nothing waiting for him.

He made his way over to his desk, noting along the way that Kate was not in yet. Spotting a manila file folder waiting for him, his hope returned. However, instead of a case file from another department, he was disappointed again, this time to find it was the Reyna neighborhood canvas reports.

With a sigh, he dropped into his chair and pulled the top sheet. The bottom line glared back at him.

The homeowner reported nothing unusual.

He pulled the next sheet.

The homeowner reported nothing unusual.

He pulled the third sheet.

The homeowner reported nothing unusual.

Though not surprised, the results only added to his sense of frustration. Sheet four was different.

The homeowner reported an unfamiliar vehicle parked in front of their home.

Tanner sat upright, his interest piqued, and quickly read the full account of the interview:

1131 S. Quitman.
Homeowner—Ward Nylander

Mr. Nylander indicated he saw a silver or gray car parked in front of his home on the night in question. He'd seen it once before but did not know exactly when.

He did not see the occupant, or write down the license plate.

146

The approximate time was 8:00 p.m., and the car was there for approx. forty-five minutes.

It was signed by the officer.

Tanner stood and went around to Kate's desk. There was still no sign of her.

"Stay away from my stapler, Austin."

Tanner turned to see her coming off the elevator.

"It's mine, and you know it."

She laughed. "Whatever."

He handed her the canvas report, which she read then handed back.

"I have news, as well. Ballistics matched the slugs from Mariel Reyna's body to the one found in Carole Hampton."

"Not a surprise, I guess. Still, it's something."

"At least we're not looking for two weapons, and it solidifies the connection between the two murders. Anything come in from around the state?"

He shook his head. "Not a single response—at least so far."

"Then I suggest we pay Mr. Nylander a visit."

He checked the sheet for a phone number. "I'll call and make sure he's home, then meet you downstairs."

"Good. I'll play chauffeur today."

Residence of Ward Nylander
South Quitman Street
West Colfax Neighborhood
West Denver
9:30 a.m.

Foreboding gray clouds had replaced the warm sun from the day before, and instead of a southerly breeze, the wind blew damp and cold from the northwest. Occasionally, snowflakes would spit out of the sky. Such abrupt transitions in weather were part of April in Colorado.

The Nylander home was across the street and one door east from the Reynas' residence. Mr. Nylander opened the door as they approached.

"Come, come. Get in out of that cold." His accent hinted at a Scandinavian heritage.

Kate smiled. "Thank you. I'm Detective Walker, and this is Detective Austin."

"Ward Nylander. Call me Ward." He led them into a cramped but cozy living room. "Would you like some coffee?"

She shook her head. "Not for me, sir."

Chilled to the bone, Tanner wasn't about to say no. "Coffee would be great."

The elderly Swede was immensely pleased. "Wonderful. Please, please—make yourselves comfortable."

As he left the room, Kate found a seat by the front window, and Tanner settled on the couch. The house was warm, a gas-log fireplace adding to the comfort and atmosphere of the clean, modestly furnished home. Tanner's gaze was drawn to the large photo resting on the mantle. The man in the photo was clearly Mr. Nylander, and Tanner assumed the woman was his wife.

Carrying a silver tray, Ward returned. "Here we go."

Despite his short stature and thinning white hair, he had large hands that held the tray firmly. Three cups accompanied a small carafe, which was flanked by a plate of honey-colored biscuits. He poured Tanner a cup and handed it to him, then he lifted the plate of treats.

"Speculaas?"

Tanner accepted the cookie. "What did you call them?"

"Speculaas. A Dutch cookie. Very good."

Still leaning over the tray, he turned to Kate.

"I brought an extra cup. Can I change your mind?"

Kate smiled, won over by the man's kindness. "Yes, I believe you can."

He poured her a cup and offered a biscuit, which she declined.

Tanner took a bite. Butter, cinnamon, and several other spices he couldn't identify filled his mouth. "Wow. These are delicious."

Ward beamed. "They're a specialty of my Elsa."

Tanner gestured toward the photo. "Is that Elsa?"

"Yes. She's at a church meeting this morning."

"Well, please tell her how much I liked her cookies."

"I will. Now, what is it I can do for you detectives?"

Kate set her coffee down. "We read a report that said you noticed an unfamiliar vehicle on the night Mariel Reyna was killed."

The man's face darkened instantly. "That is a terrible thing. Those poor people, the Reynas, and so nice, too."

150

Tanner finished his cookie and pulled out his pad. Ward did not need further prompting.

"It was very strange. He, at least I believe it was a he, parked right in front of our house and turned off all but his parking lights. He just sat there, but because there was no moon that night, I really couldn't see what he was doing."

"How long would you say he was there?"

"Forty-five minutes or so. I went to the bathroom around eight-thirty, and when I returned, he had driven off."

Kate glanced toward the photo of Elsa. "Did your wife see the car?"

"No. She had already retired for the evening."

"You mentioned the color of the car; has anything else come back to you since speaking with our officer?"

"Not really. Like I said, gray or silver, but expensive."

Tanner didn't recall that detail. "What makes you say it was an expensive car?"

"The chrome. Lots of shiny chrome that reflected our porch light."

"What about the wheels? Were they chrome?"

Ward's forehead wrinkled as he considered the question. "I believe they were. Yes, they were shiny, also."

Tanner made a note. "Is there anything else you can remember?"

"No, I'm afraid not."

Kate pulled out a business card and laid it on the coffee table. "Mr. Nylander, if you think of anything at all, regardless of how small it seems, please, call us."

"I certainly will. More coffee?"

"No, thank you."

"How about you, young man?"

Tanner glanced at his watch. The funeral for Carole Hampton was in an hour.

"I would love to accept, but we have to be somewhere very soon."

Ward stood. "I understand. Let me see you out."

Fairmount Cemetery
Quebec Street
Southeast Denver
1:55 p.m.

The second-oldest cemetery in Denver, Fairmount was a parklike 280 acres with over 3800 trees. Final resting place to over a dozen Colorado governors and an equal number of United States senators, it had sections with names like *The Garden of Honor, The Esplanade,* and *Millionaire's Row.*

In a part of the cemetery without any such formal name, Kate parked at the end of a long line of cars. From there, they watched people making their way up to a large black canopy. Kate was holding back on purpose, hoping to approach unnoticed.

Neither she nor Tanner were looking forward to the funeral; the depressing weather made the unpleasant task worse. While death notifications were the worst part of their job, attending family funerals ran a close second.

The ride over to the cemetery had been quieter than normal.

Tanner had suggested they stop to pick up some lunch, but Kate wasn't hungry, and they were short on time. Fortunately, Ward Nylander had filled Tanner's pockets with Speculaas; her partner's cookie crunching was the only noise as they sat in a somber silence.

The spitting snow of earlier had transitioned to a cold rain, further adding to their reluctance to leave the car. She checked her watch then sighed.

153

"I guess it's time."

Kate got out and opened an umbrella. When Tanner climbed out, he quickly sidled up to her in an attempt to borrow one side of the pop-up shelter. It was too small for the job.

Kate chided him. "You need to think about these things, Tanner."

"Now you tell me."

"You're a big boy, aren't you?"

He rolled his eyes and accepted the futility of trying to stay dry, relinquishing the little cover he had.

They walked slowly up the road, taking note of both the gray and the silver cars.

It seemed those two shades were the preferred color for Carole Hampton's friends and relatives. Kate counted no less than a dozen cars matching the description, chrome and all. Not only was the color description generic, but they had to interpret what Ward Nylander considered was *a lot* of chrome.

Coming in from behind the gathering, they sat in the back row of chairs. Kate took a quick count; her rough estimate was about thirty people in attendance.

She nudged Tanner. "We need to try to identify as many of these mourners as possible."

He nodded, took out his notepad, and while keeping it low around his waist, started making notations. Meanwhile, Kate scanned for someone who looked out of place.

Only one face struck her as odd, and not because it was unfamiliar. Ken Blackwell.

Kate touched Tanner's elbow and leaned in to whisper. "You see who's here?"

Tanner nodded. "Some nerve."

"Yeah, but if Hampton had no clue about the affair, Blackwell wouldn't worry about a scene."

"True, I guess. Still, it seems off."

"I agree. I'm gonna have a word with him when this is over. Will you give our sympathies to Tom Hampton?"

"Sure."

Fifteen minutes later, the service came to a close, and a line of mourners began to file past Tom, his son, and the casket. Kate had been watching Blackwell, and when he headed for his car without getting in line, she followed him.

He was at his car when she caught up to him.

"Mr. Blackwell?"

He turned, saw her, and unlocked his car. Climbing in, he shut the door then rolled the window down partway.

"Hello, Detective. Glad to see one of Denver's finest in attendance."

"You left without paying your respects."

"I'm late for an appointment at the museum."

"The DAM?"

"That's right."

Kate's adrenaline surged. "I didn't know you had a connection with the DAM."

His smile looked forced. "I trust there is much you don't know about me."

"May I ask your business there?"

"I'm on the community art board."

"The advisory board?"

"That's right. Why?"

Kate kept her expression locked. "Wasn't Carole Hampton also on that board?"

His hesitation was brief but obvious. "She was."

"And you didn't feel it necessary to mention this before?"

His eyes flashed with anger. "I didn't see why it would be important."

His window whirred up, but she stuck her notebook in the track, stopping it still cracked open.

He scowled at her. "Do you mind?"

She didn't. "One last question. Does the name Mariel Reyna mean anything to you?"

"No." He stared at her, obviously waiting to leave.

She smiled. "Do you mind?"

He didn't try to hide the hostility in his voice. "Mind what?"

"You have my pad trapped in your window."

The window dropped slightly, and she retracted the pad. He sped off.

Tanner came up behind her. "What was that about?"

"It turns out our friend Blackwell is part of the same advisory board that Carole Hampton was on."

"Really? That is interesting. Did you ask him why he hadn't mentioned that?"

"I did. He said he didn't think it was important."

"I would tend to disagree. That gives him a potential connection to our second victim."

She nodded. "Thin, but not as thin as we had before. I asked if he knew her name, and he said no. Did you notice the color of his car?"

"I did, and all that shiny chrome, as well."

"It's not my style, and neither is he, for that matter."

He grinned at her. "I didn't know you had a style."

She grunted. "Oh, I've got a style, Austin. I've got a style!"

Denver Police Department
District 2 Precinct
Holly Street
4:45 p.m.

Sitting in the conference room, Tanner pulled out his notes from the funeral and began to read the list. Kate sat opposite him, her hands in her lap, listening as he recounted the names of those he'd recognized.

"Hampton and his son, of course. Then there were the eight people who were dressed in Southwest Airlines uniforms, all female except one. The lone male was Burt Givens, who we met at the airport."

He flipped a page.

"I noted four elderly people in a small group, and when I approached, I realized it was Nettie Tiller and three of her friends."

Kate smiled. "A sweet lady. Where did the other three come from?"

"Apparently, they also lived in the neighborhood. Each had already been interviewed in the area canvas but hadn't seen anything."

"Okay. Anyone else?"

"When I went up front to pay our respects, I noticed a lapel pin on several guests in line. Curious, I asked. It turned out to be from the DAM."

Kate cocked her head to one side. "Oh? What did it signify?"

"That they were docents."

"Docents?"

"Volunteers."

"I see. Did you get names?"

"I did. Jennifer Moss, Gloria Benitez, Sarah Edwards, and Angelo Beckett."

"There were also two other individuals from the museum. A young lady by the name of Joanna Seabrooke, who's the public relations officer for the DAM, and Paul Ridley."

"What does he do?"

"He is the Museum Educator. He plans tours, develops programs for different age groups, and oversees the docents."

"Volunteers."

Tanner smiled. "Them, too."

Kate rocked forward in her chair. "We should talk to them."

"I agree. First thing tomorrow."

"Why tomorrow?"

Tanner pointed up at the clock. "They close in four minutes."

"You're always dragging your feet, Austin."

"You're my mentor. I must get it from you!"

Friday, April 10

Denver Art Museum
Civic Center Park
West 14th Avenue Parkway
Downtown Denver
10:20 a.m.

The museum was already humming with activity when Tanner and Kate arrived the next morning. Tanner found them a parking spot on Fourteenth Avenue, and they entered through the Welcome Center entrance.

They were greeted by a security guard at the desk. "Good morning."

Tanner smiled and showed his badge. "Same to you. Where are the offices?"

The guard pointed behind him. "Follow that hall back to the first door on the left."

"Thanks."

Tanner and Kate made their way to the hall, pausing to let a line of school kids file past, and then he and Kate went through a door marked *Administration*. Tanner approached the tall desk that served as a partition between the entrance and the inner workings of the office. They were greeted by a middle-aged woman who wore her gray-tinged black hair pinned up in a bun.

"Can I help you?"

He showed his badge again. "We're with Denver PD. We'd like to speak with someone about one of your employees."

"Our HR manager is on vacation. Perhaps I can find someone else."

"That would be fine. Would you like us to wait here?"

"Please."

As she went off to search for help, Tanner turned to find Kate had walked over to the far wall and was staring at a painting. He came up next to her.

"You like it?"

She scoffed. "I've never understood what passes for art."

Tanner examined the painting. It appeared to be a face, or maybe two faces, that were cut up and misplaced like puzzle pieces thrown onto the floor. He liked it.

"What do you see, Kate?"

"See? Nothing. My childhood drawings of a pony were better than this."

He laughed.

She turned to look at him. "You're going to tell me you see something in that?"

"Well, yes. It appears to be two faces that have been jumbled together in a pile, but there are only three eyes."

She squinted at him, as if she suddenly suspected him of having alien DNA. "Three eyes, huh?"

"Yeah, so I think the artist is saying that he feels torn to pieces, and even if he was put back together, something would be missing."

She looked at the picture again and then back at him. "I think *you* have something missing, Austin!"

He laughed. "You're not the first."

"When did you become an art aficionado?"

"Laura loves to paint, and so, when an interesting exhibition is in the area, I get volunteered to go along."

Kate grinned at him. "Ah, the things we do for love."

"Detectives?"

They turned to find a young lady in her late twenties. She had long brown hair and black, wide-rimmed glasses. She came over to where they stood.

"I was told you had some questions about one of our employees."

Tanner still had his badge out.

"Yes, ma'am. I'm Detective Austin, and this is my partner, Detective Walker."

"Joanna Seabrooke. I'm Public Relations Officer for the museum."

"I remember you from the funeral yesterday."

The mention of the funeral seemed to unsettle her. She looked around behind her. "Would you like to come back to my office?"

Tanner nodded. "That would be fine."

They followed her through a swinging gate and back to a glass-walled office. Inside, the décor was modern but simple and contained a desk—better described as a table—two hard-plastic chairs in front of it, and a swivel seat situated behind. A couple lithographs were the only things on the wall.

"Please, make yourselves comfortable. Can I get you something?"

Tanner declined, as did Kate.

Joanna slid into her seat and brushed her bangs to the side with a delicate hand.

"It's terrible, what happened to Carole. She was such a nice lady."

Tanner referred to his notes from the funeral.

"I saw five others from the museum at the funeral. Did they feel the same way about Mrs. Walker?"

"Yes, absolutely. She didn't have an enemy in the world, at least, not here at the museum."

"Was Mariel Reyna also liked by everyone?"

"Mariel? Why?"

Tanner and Kate exchanged glances. They both had assumed word would have gotten back to the museum about Mariel Reyna's murder. It appeared they were wrong.

Kate cleared her throat. "Miss Seabrooke..."

"Joanna, please."

"Joanna... I'm sorry to be the one to tell you this, but Mariel Reyna was found dead yesterday morning."

Tanner watched as Joanna's big, dark eyes blinked then went blank. She stared at Kate as if waiting for more information.

Kate leaned forward. "Joanna?"

Joanna's voice had assumed a flat monotone. "There must be some mistake. You're talking about Carole Hampton, correct?"

"I'm afraid not."

"Both Carole and Mariel are dead?"

"Yes."

The eyes blinked back to life and welled up. "How is that possible?"

"That's what we're investigating."

Joanna stood suddenly. "Excuse me for a minute, will you?"

She was out the door before they could respond.

Tanner looked at Kate. "I guess no one from the family called the museum."

"If they did, no one told Miss Seabrooke."

The sound of commotion from outside the office drew closer until it burst through the door. A red-haired man was following Joanna, obviously upset with her.

"What are you talking about, Joanna?"

He stopped when he saw Tanner and Kate, and Tanner recognized him from the funeral. Paul Ridley.

Joanna stood by her desk and pointed at Tanner and Kate. "Ask them."

"Ask them what?"

Kate stood and, using her most soothing voice, tried to get a hold on the situation.

"Sir, I'm Detective Walker. You are?"

"Paul Ridley."

"Would you mind shutting the door for a minute?"

Ridley looked at Joanna then obliged.

Joanna dropped into her seat and crossed her

arms. It looked to Tanner as if she was in shock.

Kate was still trying to calm Ridley.

"Can I ask what you do here at the museum, sir?"

"I'm the Museum Educator."

"And does that bring you in contact with Mariel Reyna?"

Ridley's temper flared. "Of course, it does. She's my best docent."

"Then I'm sorry to be the one to tell you this, but Mariel Reyna was found dead yesterday."

Ridley was having none of it. "Pfft. That's ridiculous. I spoke to her…"

He stopped, his gaze moving to look at Joanna. The color drained from the man's face, and Tanner suspected Ridley was about to pass out. Tanner took the man's arm and steered him to a chair.

"You want something to drink, Mr. Ridley?"

He didn't answer, but Tanner turned to Joanna anyway.

"Can we get him a glass of water?"

She jumped up, suddenly more concerned about her coworker than herself. "I'll be right back."

A few minutes later, after sipping the drink retrieved by Joanna, most of the color had returned to Ridley's face. "I don't understand. First Carole, now Mariel. It doesn't make any sense."

Kate, with her experience, took the lead. She maintained her soothing tone. "Is there anyone else here at the museum who needs to be told about Mariel Reyna?"

Ridley shrugged. "Everybody knew her."

"What about close friends or project partners? Maybe a best friend at the museum?"

A spark of realization. "Palmer."

"Palmer? Who is Palmer?"

"Thad Palmer. He's a curator. He and Mariel were working on a project for the kids' program this summer."

"A curator?"

Joanna explained. "He's in charge of collecting, cataloging, and displaying certain kinds of art."

Tanner jotted down the name. "Is he here now?"

Joanna picked up the phone. After a brief conversation, she hung up. "He's in his office."

Kate stood. "We'll go see him when we're done here. Joanna, can I speak to you outside?"

Obviously caught off guard by the request, Joanna didn't move. "Uh…"

Kate insisted. "Just for a few minutes."

Joanna pushed herself up and followed Kate to the door. Kate looked at Tanner, who had already figured out what his partner was doing. He nodded and waited for her to shut the door behind them, then he turned to Ridley.

"I need your help."

Ridley's gaze moved from the floor to look at Tanner. "Okay."

"How did you know Carole Hampton?"

"I met her at an advisory board meeting."

"The community art board?"

"That's right."

"Was there anyone she didn't get along with there?"

Ridley shook his head. "Not that I was aware of. She was always sweet to everyone."

"How would you describe your relationship with Mrs. Hampton?"

"What do you mean?"

Tanner shrugged. "Cordial, friendly, close?"

"Friendly, I guess."

"Did your relationship extend beyond the museum?"

Ridley's eyes reflected some inner turmoil. "Why would you ask that?"

169

"I just need you to answer the question. Did you two have a personal relationship?"

"No, never."

"What about Mariel Reyna?"

"What about her?"

"Did you and Mariel ever develop a personal relationship?"

"No... I mean... No."

Tanner pulled his chair a little closer. "You seem unsure, so I'll ask again. Did you and Mariel Reyna ever develop a personal relationship?"

Ridley fidgeted. "Look, it's no secret that Mariel was a pretty girl, and I told her that. But she was engaged and had no interest in me or anyone else."

"So, is it possible you made a pass at her, and when she rejected you, you snapped?"

"No! Absolutely not."

Tanner wasn't inclined to believe the man.

"Where were you last Sunday evening?"

"Easter? I attended a cantata at my church."

"What time did it end?"

Ridley shrugged. "Eight or so."

"And Wednesday night?"

"Home. I was watching the Avalanche playoff game."

Tanner made a mental note to check on the hockey game.

"Was there anyone else who may have had an interest in Miss Reyna?"

Ridley jumped at the opening. "Yeah, yeah! Beckett."

"Beckett?"

"Angelo Beckett. He's another one of my docents. He had a huge crush on Mariel."

Tanner leaned back and considered his options. He could push Ridley further and possibly lose any cooperation from the man in the future, or ease off for now to focus on Angelo Beckett. Tanner chose the latter.

"Is Beckett here today?"

"No. He called in sick."

That scratched Tanner's investigative itch. It seemed a convenient day to missing work.

"Can you get me the information on this Angelo Beckett?"

"Sure. You want me to get it now?"

"Please. Also, I'll need the name of your church."

MAD Greens
1200 Acoma Street
Denver Art Museum Campus
Downtown
12:30 p.m.

Thad Palmer had left his office by the time Kate and Tanner arrived but was due back at one o'clock; Tanner suggested this meant they had the perfect opportunity to grab some lunch. They had opted to eat at *MAD Greens* because of its location more than its food.

A locally sourced fresh food restaurant, it had salads with names like the *Genghis Kahn* and the *Mad Molly Brown*. To Tanner's surprise, the MAD in *MAD Greens* did not refer to the museum; it turned out that besides having numerous sites in Colorado, the restaurant had locations in Utah, Arizona, and Texas.

Tanner chose a Panini called the *Mad Cuban* while Kate ordered one called the *Annie Oakley.* He found the name of her sandwich fitting. They took a seat by the window and settled in to eat. Between bites,

Kate filled him in on the rest of her interview with Joanna.

"I don't think that girl will ever be the same. She couldn't grasp that two people she knew had died just days apart, never mind that they were murdered."

Tanner nodded, washing down a bite with some tea. "It's not something a person can prepare for."

"True enough. Anyway, she didn't have a clue who might want to hurt either woman. I asked her if she'd ever heard Carole Hampton express fear of her husband. She said no. I then asked her if she knew about Carole and Blackwell."

Tanner raised an eyebrow. "And?"

"Not a clue. She doubted anyone at the museum knew."

"Paul Ridley seemed ignorant of it, as well."

Kate took a long sip of Diet Pepsi. "What else did you learn?"

"Well, let's see. He said he had no personal relationship outside work with either victim. He admitted to finding Mariel Reyna attractive but denied he was angry at a rejection. However, there was someone he hurriedly threw under the bus."

Kate grinned. "Here, take this guy!"

Tanner laughed. "Something like that. He gave me the name of an Angelo Beckett who is another one of his volunteers. Mr. Beckett called in sick today."

"Interesting. Anything else?"

"Beckett attends classes at Colorado College."

Kate paused with her drink suspended in the air. "Seriously?"

"That's the information I have."

She set her cup down. "Perhaps we should do a record check on him and Mr. Ridley."

"Perhaps we should."

Kate pushed her plate away. "How was your sandwich?"

Tanner popped the last piece into his mouth. "Okay, but I know one thing for sure."

"What's that?"

"Tonight, I'm having steak and mashed potatoes for dinner!"

Office of Thad Palmer
Denver Art Museum
Hamilton Building
1:15 p.m.

Thad Palmer greeted them at the door to his office, and though his demeanor was friendly, he wasn't smiling. Kate figured someone had delivered the news about the two women.

"Please, come in."

Kate figured Palmer to be in his late forties or early fifties, with thick brown hair that fell almost to his shoulders. Tall and fit, he had hazel eyes, and golden skin—the natural tone that came with a Mediterranean heritage. She couldn't place his accent but guessed Greek.

His gray suit appeared to be off the rack, and the white shirt beneath his jacket was open at the collar. He struck Kate as the quintessential, hippie professor, right up until he spoke. Then it was immediately obvious this was no Bohemian freethinker.

"The news about both Carole and Mariel saddens me greatly. They were both such gentle souls who appreciated art and what we do here at the museum."

Kate didn't bother with presenting her badge. "I'm Detective Walker, and this is my partner, Detective Austin."

"Pleasure to meet you both. Would you like to sit?"

"Thank you."

Palmer's office overflowed with atmosphere. Not the industrious mood of hard work being accomplished but one of peaceful reflection. The lighting was lower than most similar workspaces, and though the office was large, it felt cozy.

Kate noticed Tanner pull out his notepad, a sign she was to lead. Her smile was all business.

"Thank you for your time, Mr. Palmer."

"Of course, and please, call me Thad."

"Okay. Can you tell me about your relationship with Carole Hampton?"

Before answering, he moved around behind his desk and sat down. "Well, I only knew Carole through the advisory board. I had not worked with her on any projects. She was committed, engaging, and I found her knowledge of art to be extensive."

"Do you know if she had problems with anyone on the board?"

"I don't believe so. She was kind to everyone, and folks liked her."

"When was the last time you saw Mrs. Hampton?"

"The last board meeting, I believe."

There was no tension emanating from the curator, and Kate found his accent somewhat enchanting. Unblinking in his study of her, it caused her to flush slightly, both an uncommon and uncomfortable reaction for her. She pushed herself to stay focused.

"We understood you were working with Mariel Reyna on a project."

"That's correct. It centered on the primitive drawings of early generation Native American children. We wanted it ready for this summer."

"When did you last see Mariel?"

For the first time, Thad smiled, revealing a set of perfect teeth.

"The night before she died, I guess."

She did not return his smile. "That would make you one of the last at the museum to see her alive."

"It appears so. I find it quite unsettling, really."

Tanner had been silent, but when Kate hesitated before the next question, he jumped in.

"Mr. Palmer, did you have a personal relationship with either Carole Hampton or Mariel Reyna?"

"Personal?"

"Romantic."

Kate was both surprised and impressed with the grit Tanner showed. He was learning to be direct at the right times.

Thad's gaze never left Kate.

"Detective, it is my personal code to not

date nor fraternize with any of my coworkers."

"Seems like a good code to live by. Have you always followed it?"

"All but once." His smile toward Kate broadened. "However, my code does not include people I meet *through* work."

Tanner glanced at his notes. "Are you familiar with the name Angelo Beckett?"

Palmer finally looked directly at Tanner.

"Indeed. I am unaccustomed to offering slander, Detective, but that is a most unpleasant individual."

"So, you have worked with him, is that right?"

"Once. I asked that he not be assigned to aid me again."

Tanner looked at Kate, and when she shrugged, he stood and laid a business card on the desk.

"Thank you, sir. If you think of anything, please call."

"I would be happy to." Thad turned his gaze back to Kate. "Do you also have a card, Detective Walker?"

Kate stood, regaining her footing in more than one way. "Unfortunately, I'm all out."

"Pity."

She smiled. "Isn't it?"

178

JOHN C. DALGLISH

*Office of Joanna Seabrooke
Welcome Center
Denver Art Museum
2:00 p.m.*

As they waited outside the public relations office of Joanna Seabrooke, Tanner studied his partner.

"Mr. Palmer was interested in you."

She grunted. "Whatever."

"Oh, come on. You had to notice."

"I noticed. He's a nice-looking man, I won't deny that."

Tanner curled his lip into a knowing grin. "You're not out of business cards, are you?"

"Hard to say. I haven't checked."

He laughed. "That's what I thought!"

"That's enough out of you, mister. Thad Palmer is not my type."

His grin widened. "Oh! So now you have a style *and* a type!"

She took a backhanded swipe at him, but he saw it coming.

179

"Hey! No assaulting a fellow officer!"
She glared at him. "You're familiar
with the phrase 'where angels fear to
tread'?"

"I am."

"Well, Gabriel himself wouldn't go
down the path you're treading."

Tanner held up his hands in surrender.
"Okay, okay."

The office door opened, and Joanna
came out.

"I'm so sorry for keeping you waiting.
How can I help you?"

The news from earlier in the day had
clearly taken a toll on the young woman,
and Tanner's heart went out to her. "We just
have a couple questions."

"Do you want to come in?"

The waiting area was empty, so
Tanner shook his head. "This won't take
long."

"Okay."

"What is your relationship with Thad
Palmer?"

"Thad? Friendly. He's a very nice man
and extremely intelligent."

Tanner flashed Kate an "I told you so"
look.

She ignored him and asked her own
question.

180

"Mr. Palmer indicated he does not get romantically involved with coworkers. Have you noticed if that is indeed the case?"

Her eyebrows knitted together. "I guess. I've only ever seen him be professional with the staff."

Kate sensed the young woman was holding back.

"He mentioned he'd only had a single relationship with a coworker. Do you know who that was?"

"I don't."

Tanner looked up from his notes. "What about Angelo Beckett?"

"What about him?"

"Would you describe him as someone you trust?"

"I haven't had many dealings with him, so I wouldn't feel comfortable saying."

Kate looked at Tanner and signaled she was done.

Tanner nodded. "I think that's all we need. Thank you again."

"You're welcome."

Joanna returned to her office, and Tanner followed Kate out into the rotunda. "What do you think?"

Kate shrugged. "She's hiding something."

"Yeah, but what?"

"Good question. You have Mr.
Beckett's address, so let's go ask him."

Home of Angelo Beckett
Courthouse Square Apartments
Lincoln Park Neighborhood
3:20 p.m.

Less than ten minutes west of the art
museum, Kate and Tanner found the weary
conglomeration of brick known as the
Courthouse Square Apartments. Two
buildings, one five stories and the other
eight, made up the complex. Stains on the
hallway carpet, too big to be from a dog,
spoke to a roof that had been compromised
at some time in the past. Ceiling panels
sagged, threatening to drop on them.

Angelo Beckett was on the second
floor of the eight-story tower. Number 207B
was easy enough to find, and a quick
succession of three knocks brought the noise
of shuffling feet toward them. The door
opened to reveal a guy in his late twenties or
early thirties in a ripped t-shirt, tattered

shorts, and a sweat-stained Colorado Rockies ball cap. He stared at them, apparently not interested enough to ask who they were.

Tanner moved his foot far enough forward to prevent the door from re-closing. "Angelo Beckett?"

The man nodded.

Kate produced her badge. "I'm Detective Walker. This is Detective Austin. Mind if we come in?"

"What for?"

His soprano-level voice was surprising, especially since Beckett was easily over six feet and on the heavy side of two hundred pounds.

Kate smiled. "Just want to talk."

Beckett, barefoot and bare-chested, didn't appear to be under the weather at all. "I guess."

He turned and walked back into the apartment, Tanner right behind him.

Kate closed the door behind her then joined them in the tiny living room. What little space there was had been overcome by a collection of pizza boxes and empty two-liter soda bottles. Surprisingly, beer cans did not seem to be part of the décor.

Kate put away her badge. "We were over at the museum, and they said you called in sick."

"Yeah. Bad cough." He faked a couple hacks.

"Sounds okay to me."

"Yeah, so what? Don't you ever call in sick?"

"Sure, when I'm sick."

"Whatever. I was out late last night and didn't feel like going in. I'm just a volunteer, you know."

"So I understand. A docent, if I am correct."

"That's right." Beckett dropped into the cleared spot on the couch from where he'd apparently risen but seemed unconcerned about seating for his guests.

Tanner was scanning the room. "You live here alone?"

"Yeah."

"Mind if I look around?"

"Suit yourself. I ain't done nothin' wrong."

Kate waited until Tanner had disappeared into the bedroom.

"Did you hear the news, Angelo?"

"You mean about Carole?"

Kate noted the first-name basis. "Yeah. Were you and her friends?"

"No. I mean, she was a nice lady and all, but we only spoke a few times."

"What about Mariel Reyna?"

Beckett's demeanor changed immediately. "What about Mariel?"

"I heard you have a crush on her."

"Yeah, so? Everyone at the museum knows that."

"What about in your class together. Everybody there know how you feel?"

"I imagine."

Kate focused in on his eyes, convinced he didn't know what was coming.

"Did you know Mariel was killed last night?"

The impact of the statement was physical. His eyes widened, and he rocked back against the couch. "What? Killed? No way."

Though his reaction appeared emotional, Kate was unsure if it was genuine.

"I'm afraid so."

"What happened?"

"She was murdered."

"Murdered? I can't believe it."

To Kate, it seemed as if he wasn't having as much trouble believing it as he declared.

"Where were you Wednesday night, Angelo?"

"With some friends. Wait, you don't think I had anything to do with it, do you?"

"Do these friends have names?"

He nodded. "Jennifer, Gloria, and Sarah. We went out for drinks after leaving the museum."

"Where was this outing?"

"The Fainting Goat."

"That's a bar?"

"Yeah."

"And what time did it end?"

"I don't know. One or one-thirty in the morning."

Tanner came back into the room, shaking his head.

Kate nodded, still focused on Beckett. "What were those names again?"

"Jennifer Moss, Gloria Benitez, and Sarah Edwards."

Tanner pulled his notes. "Those are the three girls you were with at the Walker funeral."

Beckett's head swiveled quickly in Tanner's direction. "Uh...yeah. We hang out a lot, and that's who I was with Wednesday."

Kate watched Tanner move over to the couch, sweep a pile of clothes and boxes onto the floor, then sit down next to Beckett. "Did Mariel buddy around with you guys, as well?"

"Once or twice. Not all the time."

Tanner leaned in close, the tension rising between the two men.

"So, here's the thing, Angelo. Can I call you Angelo?"

Beckett nodded weakly.

"Great. Anyway, as I was saying, here's the thing. I think you asked Mariel out several times, and on Wednesday night, you decided to ask her one last time."

"No... I didn't see her Wednesday night."

"And I think you went to see her at home, tried one final time to convince her she should go out with you, and when she refused, you killed her."

"No, no way. You're crazy!" Beckett turned toward Kate. "He's not framing me for this. I didn't do it."

Tanner stood and glared down at the man. "We're going to check out your alibi, and if it falls apart, I'm coming back for you. Do you understand?"

Beckett had fallen mute.

Tanner walked out, and after dropping a business card on the table, Kate followed him.

As they rode the elevator down, she stared at him.

"You think he did it?"

Tanner shrugged. "I haven't a clue. There was nothing in the bedroom that could tie him to either victim, so I thought I might scare it out of him. What about you? Do you think he's our guy?"

The elevator door opened with a ding.

"I'm not sure. I don't like him, though."

"Let me guess. He's not your style or type?"

She laughed. "Definitely not!"

When they got back to their car, Tanner placed a call to Joanna Seabrooke.

"Hello?"

"Joanna, it's Detective Austin."

"Hi, Detective. Is everything okay?"

"Yes. I'd like to run three names by you."

"Okay."

He read the names from his pad. "Jennifer Moss, Gloria Benitez, and Sarah Edwards."

"I recognize them. They're all docents."

"Are they there now?"

"I'm not sure. Do you want to hold on?"

"Yes, please."

A few minutes later, Joanna was back.

"I spoke with Paul Ridley, and he said none of them worked today. He did mention that Jennifer and Sarah will both be in tomorrow morning."

Tanner covered the phone.

"None of them are working. Two will be there in the morning. Wait or get addresses?"

"Tomorrow will work."

Tanner nodded his agreement.

"Thanks, Joanna. We'll speak to them in the morning."

When he hung up, he glanced at his watch. It was nearly five o'clock, and it had been a long day. Besides, he had an appointment with a steak-and-potatoes dinner. "Call it a day?"

Kate shook her head. "There's one other thing I want to do."

"Which is?"

"I'd like to run DMV searches on all our major players. Perhaps we can narrow things down by the cars they drive."

"Gray or silver—I like it. Maybe we should get Palmer's phone records, and try to nail down his whereabouts a little more."

"Good idea."

"Then call it a day?"

She laughed. "Done!"

DENVER HOMICIDE

Saturday, April 11

*Denver Police Department
District 2 Precinct
Holly Street
8:15 a.m.*

Two manila envelopes were waiting on Tanner's desk the next morning. He set his coffee down and dropped into his chair. The first one he opened contained Thad Palmer's phone records.

A quick scan of the top page, then the next, and the next, made one thing clear. Palmer either turned his phone off at night, or he never went anywhere. Either way, the logs were not much help.

The second envelope held the DMV printouts on each of their suspects. As they already knew, gray and silver were popular car colors with the museum crowd, and so

the printouts didn't help them narrow things
down.

"Anything good?"

Tanner looked up to see Kate had
arrived. "Not really."

"Well, we still have our appointment
at the museum, so brief me on the way. I'll
be downstairs."

He grabbed the folders. "Right behind
you."

Denver Art Museum
Civic Center Park
West 14th Avenue Parkway
Downtown Denver
10:00 a.m.

The atmosphere and hum of the
museum was similar to what Kate and
Tanner had experienced the day before, but
moods seemed to be a little lighter. Even
Tanner sensed it. The weather for the
coming weekend was to be warm and sunny,

and Spring Fever was rampant in Central Colorado.

Paul Ridley had been summoned when Tanner and Kate arrived.

He, too, was all smiles. "Good morning."

Tanner and Kate responded in unison. "Morning."

"I understand you wanted to speak with Jennifer and Sarah."

Tanner nodded. "Are they both in?"

"They are. Follow me."

They left the office and followed Ridley across the giant Ponti Hall, up a set of stairs, and into a large warehouse area, where equipment and art were stored. Voices filtered to them from the back of the room.

Ridley stopped by the door.

"Jennifer, Sarah! Got a minute?"

The talking ceased, and footsteps echoed off the walls, as the girls came to the door. Both young women were blonde, less than five feet tall, and in their twenties. They were dressed in smocks and had apparently been painting. Yellow pigment covered their hands and arms, and one of them even had it on her face. They were smiling, apparently enjoying themselves immensely.

Ridley nodded toward Tanner and Kate.

"This is Detective Austin and Detective Walker. They need to ask you a few questions."

The girls' smiles disappeared, prompting Tanner to laugh.

"It's okay, ladies. We're not here to arrest you."

The smiles returned, although more subdued.

Ridley identified the volunteers. "This is Jennifer Moss, and the one with paint on her face is Sarah Edwards."

Kate nodded. "Nice to meet you."

Jennifer, the no-face-paint girl, looked up at Paul. "Is this about Mariel?"

The educator deferred. "I'll let the detectives explain, okay?"

Both girls nodded.

After Paul excused himself, Tanner directed the girls to some chairs near the wall. Once seated, they looked up at him expectantly, radiating nervousness. Tanner suspected a trip to the principal's office was the most serious trouble either had endured.

He tried to calm them. "This won't take long, but we need you to be completely truthful, okay?"

In unison, both girls nodded again.

"Okay. We'd like you to tell us where you were on Wednesday night."

Sarah scrunched her forehead in thought, but Jennifer seemed prepared for the question.

"We went out for drinks after work."

Kate took out her notepad. "Where did you go?"

"The Fainting Goat."

"You, too, Sarah?"

She nodded. "Yeah."

"Was it just the two of you?"

Jennifer shook her head. "Gloria and Angelo were with us."

"What are their full names?"

"Gloria Benitez and Angelo Beckett."

"What time did you guys call it a night?"

Sarah's brow furrowed again, but Jennifer was ready. "Around one...maybe one-thirty."

"And you all left together?"

"Yeah."

Tanner had been watching Sarah, and something appeared to be troubling her. She was rubbing absently at the yellow paint on her face, and her eyes grew wide when he bent over to look at her directly.

"Does that sound right, Sarah?"

"I'm not sure."

"You're not sure about what?"

"Well, I think we left earlier than that." She turned to her friend. "Weren't we home by 1:30, Jenn?"

"I don't think so."

Tanner's shifted his focus to Jennifer, zeroing in on the girl who suddenly couldn't get comfortable in her seat.

"So think hard, Jennifer. Is it possible you may have left the bar before 12:30?"

She gave an unconvincing shrug. "It's possible, I guess. I really can't say for sure."

"Were you girls aware that Angelo was interested in Mariel?"

Both girls nodded.

Sarah sighed. "That was one of the reasons Mariel rarely went out with us after work."

"What was?"

"She didn't feel comfortable around Angelo. He was always hitting on her, and she'd made it clear she wasn't interested."

Jennifer took exception to her friend's assertion. "That was over. Angelo had moved on. There was someone else he was interested in."

Sarah dismissed the suggestion. "Whatever."

Kate put away her pad and smiled down at Sarah. "Thanks for your help. Can you give us a moment with Jennifer?"

Sarah's yellow-stained face took on an uncertain expression; she appeared as if she was afraid to abandon her friend. Finally, she stood. "Of course."

Once Sarah was out of earshot, Kate sat down next to Jennifer.

"Jennifer, is it all right if I ask you a personal question?"

"Uh... I guess."

"When you say Angelo had moved on to someone else, did you mean yourself?"

Tanner wasn't sure if he or Jennifer was more surprised by Kate's question. The girl appeared as if she was about to cry. "Yes."

"Do you have a crush on Angelo?"

"Yes."

"Have you two dated?"

"We've talked about it."

"Did you talk about it last night?"

Jennifer nodded.

Kate stood. "Thank you, Jenn. You can go back with Sarah now."

The girl beat a path back to where her friend was while Kate headed out into the hall.

Tanner followed, and the two of them leaned on a railing, casually watching the crowd of school kids below. A pair of teachers was trying to shepherd their rambunctious group through a doorway while attempting not to lose any of their charges.

Tanner rotated and leaned backward against the railing.

"How did you pick up on the Jenn-Angelo connection?"

She shrugged. "Call it a girl thing."

"You think her story was rehearsed?"

"Probably."

"It matches Beckett exactly."

She nodded. "Sometimes, the stories match perfectly because they're true."

"But if Sarah is right about leaving earlier, then Beckett has a problem."

"I guess we should visit the Fainting Goat."

Tanner checked his watch.

"It will probably be time to eat when we get there."

She laughed. "It's always time for you to eat, Austin!"

The Fainting Goat Pub Capitol Hill District South Denver 11:10 a.m.

On the fringes of downtown, stuck in amongst numerous retail shops, the unassuming Fainting Goat Pub was three stories of Irish pub character. The long, polished bar on the ground floor faced wooden steps that led up to a second level and then up one more flight to a rooftop patio. Patrons could challenge a friend to a game of darts or play tabletop shuffleboard.

The combination of it being Friday and lunchtime meant it was busy, but the establishment had charm and atmosphere, prompting Tanner to wonder why he'd never been there.

Apparently, they looked out of place because a waitress rerouted herself and approached them immediately.

"Can I help you find something?"

Kate flashed a badge. "The manager?"

"Straight ahead, last booth."

"Thanks."

Tanner followed Kate, and at the indicated booth, they found a man in his late thirties or early forties. He sported a t-shirt and ball cap, both declaring he had been *Trapped at the Goat*.

Kate made her badge reappear. "I'm Detective Walker. This is Detective Austin. We're with Denver PD. Are you the manager?"

"I am. Name's Ollie Loomis."

"Can we have a minute of your time, Mr. Loomis?"

He had an easy smile and a kind face. "Of course. You want to sit down?"

"Perhaps in a moment. Do you have a surveillance system?"

"Sure."

"We need to verify an alibi, and your video could be very helpful."

"When do you need to see?"

"Wednesday night, between midnight and closing."

Loomis slid out from the booth and stretched. "It'll take me twenty minutes or so to cue it up. You want a drink?"

Kate smiled. "Thanks, but not while we're on duty."

Tanner had another idea. "Mind if we grab a bite to eat?"

Loomis smiled. "Not at all. Here, use my booth, and I'll send you a waitress."

A few minutes later, Tanner dug in to a giant burger that went by the name of *The Steamboat*, while Kate had ordered fish tacos. Tanner's burger, which featured poblano peppers and chipotle mayo, tasted like heaven.

Kate laughed. "I take it you like your burger more than yesterday's panini."

"Oh, man. This thing is phenomenal!"

They ate in silence for another ten minutes, but Loomis still hadn't returned by the time they finished. With the plates cleared and fresh coffee in front of them, Tanner studied his partner.

Kate quickly noticed. "What?"

"Nothing."

"Then quit staring."

He smiled. "Well, okay, it is something."

"So out with it."

"What did you think when Frank told you I was going to be your new partner?"

Kate's eyes gave away her surprise at the question. "You really want to know?"

"I do."

"I thought about how I didn't want to wet-nurse another detective."

Tanner was neither surprised nor offended. "I can't blame you for that. Do you want to know my reaction when I was told you would be training me?"

"I guess you're going to tell me, right?"

"I was a nervous wreck."

"Let me guess. The whole 'Steel Maiden' thing."

He laughed. "That may have been a part of it but mostly because I'd heard of your intensity and about your tendency to run roughshod over suspects and partners, alike."

She met his gaze. "So, is it true?"

"Yes and no, but that's not my point."

"Oh, so there *is* a point to this conversation."

He smiled at her jab. "Indeed. You see, at the time, I decided to read up on some of your cases to try to get a better idea of what I was really getting into."

"Sounds like tedious reading."

"Not at all, and I came to an interesting conclusion."

"And what was this earth-shattering deduction?"

"That you were human."

She laughed. "You could have pinched me and discovered that."

"Sure, but it was more than that. You aren't made of steel, but in fact, you are the best at your job because you care as much or more than anyone else around you."

Kate averted her eyes, and Tanner could tell he'd struck a chord.

It wasn't that she was about to get all weepy, but Tanner sensed her unease at being analyzed in such a personal way.

"What provided you with this supposed insight?" Her voice suddenly had a softer quality to it.

"One case, mostly."

"Oh? Which one?"

"The Noland case."

Kate's eyes flashed with memories, both good and bad. "I see."

"That was some tenacious and instinctive police work."

"Nice of you to say so. The mother's death was rough, but finding Missy was the highlight of my career."

"What actually happened?"

Kate sat back in her chair, and her focus seemed to move far away into the past. "Nancy Noland was murdered in her home, and her four-year old daughter was taken. Mr. Noland found his wife, and, as always, we looked at the husband as our first suspect. His alibi was rock solid, so after clearing him, we focused on the forensic evidence."

As if telling the story required a boost of energy, she paused to take a long gulp of coffee.

"A collection of hairs on the carpet near the front door turned out to be from a dog, and there was also a bowl with water in the entryway. The Nolands didn't own a dog, and the hairs didn't match any of the neighborhood animals. It occurred to me that the dog might have been a ruse to gain entrance to the home, say, for a drink of water. My gut said that anyone who could kill a woman the way Mrs. Noland was murdered probably wasn't a pet lover, so I sent the hairs off for testing."

Tanner raised an eyebrow. "Testing? You already knew they were dog hairs."

"True, but it turned out that canine DNA could reveal the breed."

"No kidding?"

"That's what I said. Anyway, the dog was a mutt, with several different breeds in its bloodline, but was predominately German shepherd. So, I called all the local pounds to see if I could get information on recent adoptions that matched."

"How many dog pounds were there?"

She smiled. "About a dozen. The pets of Denver have a lot of friends."

"You probably thought it was a longshot, at best."

"Oh, yeah. So did everyone I told."

"But it wasn't"

Kate was smiling proudly, seemingly engrossed in recounting the tale.

"Nope. Several families adopted similar dogs in the week prior to the murder, but one adoption was to a single man, just the day before Mrs. Noland was killed. Turned out he had to give a driver's license to adopt, so the address and name were genuine. When we visited his mobile home, he was extremely nervous and refused our request to search the trailer."

"Was the dog still there?"

She shook her head.

"We later found it buried in the back yard. Anyway, Reggie Grissom was taken downtown for questioning while I got a search warrant. An hour later, I found Missy Noland safe."

His partner's face beamed with the adrenaline from reliving the case. Much of what Kate had just told him was in the case file, but reading it was not like seeing it in her eyes.

"Do you know what ever happened to the little girl?"

Kate smiled broadly.

"In fact, I do. She's doing great."

Tanner shook his head slowly. "I hope I get to make a difference like that just once. It must have felt great."

"It most certainly did."

Finally, Loomis reappeared. "Sorry, Detectives. I had a devil of a time finding the correct video. Follow me."

Kate followed Loomis into a hallway, and Tanner brought up the rear. Without warning, she stopped and turned, forcing Tanner to stop suddenly.

Her eyes met his. "I know what you were doing back there."

Tanner tried to feign innocence. "What?"

Kate wasn't buying. She smiled warmly. "Thanks."

Without saying more, she turned and caught up with Loomis.

At the last door on the left, the manager turned into a small office. A single video monitor was set up on a folding table that served as a desk, and a bank of machines hummed off to one side. Loomis pointed toward the screen.

"The problem was I could only look at one camera angle at a time. We have seven cameras around the place."

Tanner assured him it was no problem. "What do you have?"

"Well, this is the main exit on Broadway. I have it cued up to midnight on Wednesday."

"Great. Let it roll."

The three stood and watched the video move slowly forward, the playback speed only slightly faster than real time, until a Colorado Rockies ball cap moved toward the door. The man beneath it was obviously Angelo Beckett; right behind him were three young women.

"Freeze it there." Tanner checked the time on the lower right of the frame. "12:36. Can you print that for us?"

Loomis nodded then hit a couple buttons. A printer in the corner started whirring then spit out a picture, which Kate retrieved.

Tanner thanked Loomis, and he and Kate headed for the car.

"The video backs up his story, to an extent."

Kate shielded her eyes against the sun as they left the bar. "Sure, but leaving the bar at 12:30 still gives Beckett time to get there and kill Mariel during the TOD timeframe."

"You don't sound convinced."

"Because I'm not. We still need to run records checks on Ridley and Beckett."

He agreed. "Back to the precinct, then?"

"Unless you have another idea."

"Nope. Fresh out. Let's go."

Denver Police Department
District 2 Precinct
Holly Street
2:45 p.m.

Standing with her feet apart and arms crossed, staring over Tanner's shoulder, Kate watched Angelo Beckett's file come up on the screen. Just like the clean report they'd found on Ridley, nothing much showed up on Beckett. A speeding ticket and a drug arrest. The drug bust occurred before the days of legalization and was for a tiny amount of marijuana in his vehicle.

She groaned. "Nothing to hang our hat on there."

"True statement."

Frank's voice carried across the squad room. "Detective Walker?"

"Over here, Lieutenant."

He rotated in their direction. "I need you and Austin in the conference room in five minutes, and bring your case files."

"Yes, sir."

Tanner looked up at Kate. "Time to explain the lack of an arrest?"

Kate shook her head. "No, probably not. He just wants to know where we are on things. Don't bother with Ridley's file, but print off Beckett's, and bring it with you. I'll get the rest."

"Okay, see you in five."

****

Five minutes turned into fifteen, as the printer decided to go on the fritz just then. Eventually, Tanner made it into the conference room, where Frank was sitting at one end of the table and Kate at the other. He slid the copy of Beckett's file to Kate then grabbed a chair.

"Sorry, Lieutenant. I had to do some copier repair."

Kate added the file to the stack of papers in front of her. "I've been laying out our suspects. Frank wanted to see them on the board."

Tanner looked up at the whiteboard on the wall at Kate's end of the room.

Paul Ridley—Museum Educator
Angelo Beckett—Volunteer
Chad Palmer—Museum Curator
Ken Blackwell—Board Member

Kate looked down at her paperwork and started working through the list.

"First, Paul Ridley. His connection to both Carole Hampton and Mariel Reyna is solid. He's a member of the art advisory board, where he served with Carole Hampton…"

Frank stopped her. "Advisory board?"

"Yeah. It's a group comprised of leaders from the DAM and volunteers from the community. The purpose is to promote a back-and-forth of ideas that would connect the museum with the people of Denver."

"And our first victim was on the board as a community member?"

Kate nodded. "She'd only been on it about six months. She was also a docent—a fancy name for a volunteer—which put her under Ridley's leadership."

"Okay. What is Ridley's connection to our second victim?"

"Mariel Reyna was also a docent, and Ridley was her direct supervisor. She was apparently his personal assistant and one of the best on his team."

"What about alibis for the nights involved?"

Tanner flipped open his notepad.

"On the night Carole Hampton was killed, Ridley was seen at a church cantata, which started at seven and ended around eight. That left insufficient time for him to commit the murder afterward. However, we cannot account for his time prior to the church musical, which means his whereabouts is unknown during part of the TOD window. The night Mariel Reyna was killed, he claimed to be home watching a hockey game and then asleep."

Tanner looked at Kate. "You have the vehicle records?"

"Yeah. A witness may have seen our killer parked, stalking Mariel Reyna. He said the vehicle was an expensive gray or silver car. Ridley drives a red pickup."

Frank sighed. "Okay. Who's next?"

Kate tapped the second name on the board. "Angelo Beckett. He's a volunteer at the museum, which brought him into contact with both Carole Hampton and Mariel Reyna, but his connection with Mariel Reyna was particularly troubling."

"How so?"

"We know he asked her out many times, and she even avoided socializing with other volunteers when she knew he would be around."

Frank raised an eyebrow. "Would his interest go to the level of stalking?"

"We don't know, and he does own a silver Chevy, though I wouldn't refer to it as expensive."

Tanner retrieved the paper of Beckett's record. "He's had a minor scrape with law enforcement but nothing to indicate this level of violence."

Kate was shaking her head. "We have a bigger problem, though. If Beckett knew Carole Hampton, it was only in passing. We can't find anything that ties them together in a significant way. Also, he has an alibi of sorts for the night of Mariel's killing."

Frank rubbed his temples. "Of sorts?"

"He was at a bar with some friends but left earlier than he claimed. We still haven't been able to nail him down on the remainder of his night."

"Next?"

"Chad Palmer. He's the curator at the museum and the last one of her associates to see Mariel alive—that we know of, anyway. They were working on a project together, but we can find no evidence of a relationship beyond the confines of the museum. Also, Mr. Palmer is the head of the advisory board, which gives him contact with Carole Hampton."

Frank appeared hopeful. "What's he drive?"

"A silver Lexus."

"Interesting. Why isn't he our guy?"

Kate held up a video disc. "This footage is from the Perry light rail station. It shows Mariel Reyna alive and getting off the train, long after she had left the presence of Thad Palmer. We've also run his phone records to try to put him near her home or the home of Carole Hampton, but either he wasn't there, or his phone was off. If he was in the area, we need another way to put him there."

Frank pointed at the whiteboard. "So far, everyone is tied to the museum. Is that the case with the last name?"

"Yes. Ken Blackwell is a neighbor to Carole Hampton and was her instructor at Colorado College, where Mrs. Hampton was taking a night course. In addition, Blackwell was on the advisory board."

Frank groaned. "I'm sensing a pattern here, Kate."

"Yes, sir. In the case of Mr. Blackwell, we discovered he had shown up at the crime scene on the night of Carole Hampton's murder. When questioned, he confessed to having an affair with Mrs. Hampton."

"But?"

"But we can find zero connection between Blackwell and Mariel Reyna. We can't even prove they knew each other."

Frank squinted at the board. "What about husbands? Either victim married?"

Tanner nodded. "Both. Mariel Reyna's husband is in the military and was overseas. Tom Hampton, Carole's husband, has been cleared. We've also cleared Michael Hampton, the first victim's stepson."

Frank sat forward and leaned on the table. "DNA? Hair? Anything?"

Kate shook her head. "Whoever our guy is, he's very careful."

Frank looked at Tanner. "What are the odds this guy will strike again?"

"I'd say nearly a hundred percent. The only thing we don't know is where."

"What about prior attacks? Has he done this before?"

"I sent out a case description to the entire state. So far, nothing."

"What about nationally?"

"That's next, I suppose."

Frank sighed and looked at Kate.

"So all we have is a group of possibles. Is that the size of it, Kate?"

She shrugged. "I'm afraid so. We need something to break free."

Frank tossed a small bag onto the table. "Perhaps this will help."

Tanner immediately recognized the particles from the Reyna scene. "Did CBI identify them?"

"They did. There from something called a Conté. It's a specialized drawing crayon—in this case, a black one."

"What do they mean by specialized?"

Frank stood and looked down at Tanner.

"If I answered that, then I'd be doing your job, wouldn't I? Then you wouldn't be needed here, would you? Then I'd have to let you go. You don't want to make me let you go, do you, Austin?"

Tanner grinned. "No, sir."

"Good. Get back to work, and let me know of any new developments."

After Frank had left the room, Kate grinned at Tanner, letting her voice drop to Frank's mocking tone.

"You don't want to make me let you go, do you, Austin?"

"Shut up, Kate!"

* * * * * * *

Kate sat at her desk with Tanner behind her, his back against the wall. She opened her computer and pulled up a Google search: *Conté*.

She got a long list of people with the last name Conté.

She added the word "crayon" and tried again. Even though Tanner was looking over her shoulder, she read the results aloud.

"Conté, also known as Conté sticks or Conté crayons, is a drawing medium composed of compressed powdered graphite or charcoal, mixed with a wax or clay. They are normally square in cross-section."

Tanner came off his leaning post and hovered where he could see the photos accompanying the description. "A drawing medium. I can't say I'm surprised."

"Me, neither, but does it help us? Both victims have a connection to art, so the crayon particles could easily have been there *before* the killings."

"Yeah, so we need to visit both homes. If we find these crayons, then we have our answer."

Residence of Mr. & Mrs. Reyna
South Quitman Street
West Colfax Neighborhood
West Denver
4:45 p.m.

The Reynas' home now carried an aura of loss, and understandably so. Whether it was his imagination or not, Tanner sensed a dark cloud around the home.

He knocked on the door, stepped back next to Kate, and waited. In a few moments, the door slowly opened, almost as if the person inside was afraid of what else might come through to hurt them.

Mr. Reyna, his hair mussed and with bags under his eyes, nodded with recognition.

"Hello, Detectives. Would you like to come in?"

Kate nodded. "If you don't mind."

"No, of course not."

Tanner followed his partner into the dimly lit hallway, the familiar layout now echoing the sadness of its residents. In the living room, a somber-faced Mrs. Reyna looked up hopefully.

"Did you find out who killed my daughter?"

Kate sat next to the woman and took her hand. "Not yet, I'm afraid. I won't give up, though; I promise."

Mrs. Reyna stared into Kate's eyes then patted her hand. "I know you won't. You're a good soul, Detective Walker."

Tanner watched the impact of the elderly woman's words on his partner. Kate eyes moistened as she smiled. "Thank you for saying so."

Mr. Reyna looked at Tanner. "Is there something else then?"

"Yes, sir. We would like to look around Mariel's bedroom again, if that's okay."

"Sure. Follow me."

Tanner glanced at Kate, who seemed unwilling to let go of Mrs. Reyna's hand. He started after Mr. Reyna. "I'll take a look around and let you know if I see anything."

Kate nodded but didn't get up. "Okay."

Tanner fell in behind Mr. Reyna as he climbed the stairs and at the top landing pushed open his daughter's bedroom door. The elderly man stepped aside.

"I'll wait downstairs with my wife and Detective Walker."

"Thank you, sir."

Tanner had visited the bedroom on the day of the murder but hadn't found anything unusual to bag as evidence. This time, he was looking for something specific, and he worked methodically from one end of the room to the other.

The room had been left untouched, giving it the sensation of a place frozen in time. Most of what he found was the same as the first time he'd looked around, but in the bottom drawer of a small dresser, he found a collection of art supplies.

Among other things, he spotted colored pencils, pads of paper, erasers, charcoal sticks, scissors, and graphite pencils. No crayons.

He stood and went to the top of the stairs. "Kate?"

She appeared at the bottom. "Got something?"

"Maybe. Can you get some evidence bags, and give me hand up here?"

"Back in a minute."

While she went to the car, Tanner put on a new set of gloves and began to remove one item at a time.

Forty-five minutes later, they had a large collection of bagged items, each one identified with permanent marker writing on the outside. While Tanner took the evidence out to their car, Kate said goodbye to the Reynas. After a few minutes, Kate joined him.

She glanced at the evidence bags.

"I didn't see any crayons."

"Nope. Everything but."

"I asked the Reynas when the funeral for Mariel was going to be held."

"And?"

"It's being delayed until Mariel's boyfriend can get back from overseas."

"That's nice of them to wait."

"I thought so."

Tanner pulled away from the curb, and they rode in silence for a while. Eventually, he looked over at Kate, who seemed lost in thought.

"You were really good with Mrs. Reyna, Kate."

She smiled, but it was a sad smile.

"Thanks. I try to put myself in their place."

Tanner wondered if it was a natural instinct or something that had come from being a long-time homicide detective. Either way, her compassion was something he hoped to have.

His phone rang. "This is Austin."

"Detective Austin, this is Thad Palmer. We met at the museum yesterday."

Tanner flashed a look at Kate. "Of course, Mr. Palmer. What can I do for you?"

"Well, this is not about business. I'm actually calling on a personal matter."

"I see."

"I was hoping you could give me Miss Walker's phone number."

"You want to get in touch with my partner?"

Kate's eyes widened, giving Tanner a sense of panic in her. He opted to play along with Palmer and torture Kate.

"Gee, I don't know, Thad. May I call you Thad?"

Palmer had barely given him the time of day on Friday but now acted as if he was Tanner's oldest buddy.

"Of course. May I call you Tanner?"

"Sure. So, Thad, would it be improper of me to ask why you need Kate's number?"

Tanner found Palmer's fake chuckle annoying.

"Well, you know how it is. I'd rather not say, but I can assure you my intentions are honorable."

Kate was doing her best to menace Tanner with her eyes. Tanner began to consider the possible consequences of incurring her further wrath.

"Look, Thad, here's what I can do. I'll let her know you called and asked about her, and then she can get in touch with you herself. Okay?"

"Sure, that's fine. You have my number?"

"It's on my phone. I've gotta run."

"Bye and thanks."

Tanner hung up, then pinned himself against the driver's door in order to avoid the hard right hand coming his way.

He grinned at her. "Cut it out, Kate! I didn't give him your number."

"I heard, and it's a good thing, too!"

"Oh, come on. He couldn't be the worst possible date you've ever had."

"I told you. He's not my type."

"Okay, okay, but…"

"Don't say it, Austin."

He laughed but heeded her warning.

DENVER HOMICIDE

Home of Tom & Carole Hampton
Montbello Neighborhood
Northeast Denver
7:25 p.m.

Tanner had called ahead to make sure Tom Hampton was home. Despite Tom's assurance that he would be there, the home was dark when they drove up. At the front door, Tanner knocked hard three times. A distant voice answered.

"It's open!"

He and Kate exchanged wary glances, then he tried the handle. As proclaimed, it gave easily, and Tanner pushed the door open just a crack.

"Mr. Hampton?"

"In here."

Tanner pushed the door open wide and led the way, Kate close behind. Tanner resisted the urge to pull his weapon, but despite the odd welcome, he saw no reason to be wary of Tom Hampton.

They found him sitting in the dark, a lone candle flickering on the coffee table, illuminating several empty beer bottles around it. Low in the background, Tanner picked up some music coming from a small speaker. The song was familiar, but he couldn't remember where he'd heard it before. As he listened to the haunting lyrics, a deep sadness weighed on him.

> *We could never see tomorrow,*
> *But no one said a word about the sorrow,*
> *How can you mend a broken heart?*
> *Please help me mend my broken heart, and let me live again.*

Tom's bloodshot eyes and dried tears were evident, even in the darkness.

Tanner sat on a chair across from the man.

"Anyone else here with you, Tom?"

He shook his head. "Just me. The airline gave me some leave for a couple weeks, so I've been spending most of the time alone."

"Do you need anything?"

"Nah. I'm makin' it."

"Tom, we know Carole enjoyed art. Did she have a studio or place where she liked to draw?"

"The study."

Tanner recalled the easel.

"May we take a look around?"

"Sure."

Kate was still by the entrance to the living room and led the way. She flipped a light switch just inside the study, blinding them both temporarily. The small area that took up one end of the room and was devoted to drawing did not reveal any significant evidence at first.

Then Kate pointed at a little tray on the floor. "You see those?"

Tanner nodded. "Crayons."

This time, he had brought several evidence bags with him, and it wasn't long before he and Kate were filling them. Most of the items were pencils, charcoal sticks, and paper, but the Conté sticks were by far the most interesting.

When they were satisfied they'd collected everything, they returned to the living room. The melancholy song was playing, probably restarted by Tom for the hundredth time, and he held a fresh beer.

"Find anything?"

"We did." Tanner held up one of the bags. "We're taking Carole's art supplies in for testing."

The man didn't seem interested in why the art items were targeted. "Fine."

"Call me if you need anything, okay, Tom?"

"Sure. Thanks."

"We'll let ourselves out."

"Good."

They left him as they found him, sitting in the darkened room, his music serving as his only comfort. Tanner wished he could do more but had no idea what.

"Sometimes, there's nothing you can do." Kate had apparently read his mind. "They just need time to work through it."

Walking back to the car in silence, Tanner tried to focus on what they'd collected.

He suggested they'd struck gold.

"These could be big. If they match the ones found at the Reyna home, we would have another connection between the two murders."

She climbed into the car. "They won't match."

He got in and stared at her. "What?"

"The crayons won't be a match."

"How can you tell?"

"Look at the bag. What do you see?"

Tanner held it up in front of his face, staring hard at the contents.

"I'm not sure. Obviously, you see something I don't."

She smiled. "Let me rephrase the question. What are you not seeing in the bag?"

He stared some more, and then it hit him. "No black!"

"Exactly. Those are all colored. The bag contains no black Contés."

"And black is what was found at the Reyna crime scene."

"Bingo."

Tanner slumped in the passenger seat. "Crap!"

Kate nodded. "Crap, indeed."

<u>Sunday, April 12</u>

Apartment of Tanner Austin
Five Points District
North Denver
11:00 a.m.

After searching both crime scenes for the black Conté crayons, Kate had told Tanner she had plans for Sunday that did not include seeing him or working on the case. Tanner had been more than happy to have some time to spend with Laura.

His fiancée was feeling somewhat neglected, as well as a little overwhelmed with the wedding planning. Her black hair was pulled back in a ponytail, and though she had no makeup on, she still looked to him as if she was ready for a night on the town.

Tanner's apartment was in the Five Points neighborhood, just north of downtown Denver. Close to bars and restaurants, it was a great area for a bachelor. Of course, he wouldn't be one much longer, and Laura had convinced him to move farther from downtown.

They were curled up on his sectional, the TV on in the background, and the Sunday crossword puzzle in their laps. Laura was stuck on a clue.

"Five letter word for attractive."

"Laura."

She batted her eyes, a reaction he wasn't sure was intentional or natural, then smiled.

"Thank you, sir. However, this has a Y as the last letter."

"Pretty."

"That's it! So simple."

The news on TV inserted itself into the conversation. A reporter, standing in front of the precinct on Holly Street, was reading from her notes.

"Police are looking into several connections between victims Carole Hampton and Mariel Reyna. The detective in charge, Kate Walker, declined to say what those connections might be…"

Tanner hit the power button, making the reporter vanish.

228

"There's a reason she doesn't want to discuss the connections—we can't find any."

Laura looked up at him.

"I thought you had them both involved with the DAM."

"We do, but none of our suspects can be tied solidly with both deaths. Everyone seems to have a solid alibi for one killing or the other."

"So, maybe they're not connected."

He shrugged. "The MOs are too similar for the cases not to be connected. We're missing something, but I don't know what. It's such a roller coaster of emotion."

"How so?"

"Well, take yesterday, for instance. We discovered a substance at the second crime scene, and it came back identified as pieces of a Conté..."

"I love those. They're great for portraits."

"Anyway, we searched both of our victims' homes in the hopes of finding those crayons. At the second location, we did."

"That's good, right?"

"We thought so, and we were pumped, until Kate realized the particles from the crime scene were from a black Conté, and the crayons we found at the home were every color but. It would have tied our scenes together and possibly locked in one of our suspects, but nope."

"And that was the letdown?"

"Big time."

Laura crossed her arms. "Well, I can tell you one thing."

"What's that?"

"Conté crayons are not an amateur's first choice for drawing. They're difficult to master. If your killer is using them, he probably has some drawing expertise."

Tanner considered his suspects in light of her suggestion.

Blackwell taught art classes. He could easily have used the Conté medium before.

Beckett was more likely to have stolen the crayon and used them out of convenience, but that seemed unlikely.

Palmer was a curator, but Tanner didn't know if Thad was also an artist.

And Ridley was Museum Educator, but that didn't mean he knew how to draw.

Tanner looked up to see Laura watching him and realized she had said something.

He attempted to apologize by way of a sheepish grin.

"I didn't mean to tune you out. What did you say?"

"I asked, are any of your suspects artists?"

"I know at least one is. He's an art teacher."

"What about the others?"

"Let's see. I've got a docent, the museum educator, and the museum curator."

She knitted her brows together, and despite the serious nature of the discussion, he found her irresistible. Leaning over, he kissed her, but she was having none of it.

"What kind?"

He raised an eyebrow. "What kind of what?"

"Museums the size of the DAM don't have *one* curator—they have *many*. What does the person on your list curate?"

He didn't know, and the look on his face apparently told her that. She crossed her arms and stared at him. "You need to find out, Tanner."

"I will, first thing in the morning."

"Good."

"Now, can I get a kiss?"

Her arms uncrossed, and her voice softened. "Well... I suppose."

DENVER HOMICIDE

Monday, April 13

Denver Police Department
District 2 Precinct
Holly Street
8:20 a.m.

Kate had not yet made her appearance
when Tanner sat down at his desk on
Monday morning. His first task, supplied by
Laura, was to learn what type of art Thad
Palmer curated.

Opening up his computer, he searched
for the staff listings at the DAM and
eventually discovered ten different areas
overseen by a chief curator. Thad Palmer
was not one of them.

Surprised, Tanner tried a different tact
in his search. He typed in Palmer's name in
conjunction with the Denver Art Museum.
This time, he found what he was looking for.

Again, he was surprised.

Thad Palmer was an *adjunct* curator in the department of Modern and Contemporary Art. His specialty jumped off the screen, sending Tanner's adrenaline surging.

Drawings.

He clicked on Palmer's museum bio and determined this guy's college loans must be astronomical.

His degrees were listed:
Bachelor of Arts from Stanford
Masters in Art History from UCLA
Ph.D. in American Art from Princeton.

He'd served as a professor at the University of Chicago and as a curator at the smaller Amon Carter Museum of American Art in Fort Worth Texas. He'd joined the DAM a little over a year ago.

Tanner pulled up the phone number for the Carter Museum in Texas and dialed.

"Amon Carter Museum. How can I help you?"

"My name is Detective Austin with the Denver Police Department. I'd like to speak with someone about a former member of your staff."

"Okay. Please hold."

Tanner stared at the picture of Thad Palmer, a business portrait posted next to his bio on the screen. Something about the man began to gnaw at Tanner, but he couldn't pin it down.

"Human Resources. This is Annette Morris."

"Good morning. My name is Detective Austin with the Denver PD. I was hoping you could give me some information on one of your former curators."

"Which one would that be?"

"Thad Palmer."

There was a brief pause. "I'll help if I can, but as I'm sure you know, much of what is in our records is confidential without a warrant."

"I understand."

"What did you want to know?"

"Did Mr. Palmer get along with his coworkers?"

"Yes, I believe so."

"What about his superiors?"

"As far as I know, his working relationship with everyone was good."

"Did Mr. Palmer leave the museum on good terms?"

A tone of reluctance worked its way into her voice. "His departure from the Amon was a mutual decision agreed to by both parties."

"That's very diplomatic, Miss Morris. Did Mr. Palmer leave the museum prior to his contract expiring?"

"I can't say."

"Is there anyone Mr. Palmer worked with that you would suggest I speak with?"

"Elaine Prentiss."

Tanner made a note. "And who is she?"

"A former docent here."

"Former?"

"Yes, sir."

"I suppose you can't reveal anything about her departure, either."

"That's correct. I do have her number in my records, though. Would you like it?"

"Yes, please."

She put him on hold then returned several minutes later. After reading off the number, she made it clear she wanted the conversation over. "I really must get back to work."

"I understand. Thank you very much for your help."

"Not at all."

The line went dead, so Tanner punched in the number for Elaine Prentiss.

"Hello?"

He was two for two now. "Is this Elaine Prentiss?"

"Yeah. Who's this?"

"My name is Detective Austin with the Denver Police Department. Do you have a minute to answer a few questions?"

Her response was immediate and startling. "What did that jerk do now?"

Tanner was caught off guard. "I'm sorry?"

"Thad Palmer. He's why you're calling, right?"

"Yes, but how did you know?"

"He's the only one I know in Denver, especially the only one who would be in trouble with the cops."

"Can I ask why you say that?"

Her anger was palatable, even over the phone.

"Thad and I began seeing each other when we met at the museum. The Amon had a strict 'no fraternization' policy, but we were very discreet. Anyway, from the very start of the relationship, he'd pushed me to pose for a drawing."

Tanner's heartrate spiked. "What kind of drawing?"

"A portrait, but I put him off. He wanted me topless, and I just wasn't comfortable with it at that point."

"So what happened?"

"We dated for several months, and finally, I relented. He kept telling me he only drew special people, and I was one of the rare individuals who met his criteria."

"Did you pose?"

"No. When he went out to his car to get his art bag, a text message showed up on his phone, and I snuck a peek. It was from another woman, wondering when he was going to draw her!"

Tanner was writing as fast as he could but kept falling behind because the details were matching his crime scenes, which forced his mind to wander.

"So what did you do?"

"I grabbed his phone and went to the front door. As he was coming back from the car, I threw it at him and told him to go draw her instead."

"And he left?"

"He did."

"I can see why you're angry."

When she continued, her voice had gone up two octaves.

"That wasn't the worst of it! I decided to get even, so I reported our relationship to the directors of the museum. You know what happened?"

"I can guess."

"Well, if your guess is I got blacklisted, you'd be right. Thad said it was my imagination, and that I'd been harassing him, and they bought it. At least publicly."

"I understood he left the museum, as well."

"Yeah, six months later when his contract was up. He moved on to a prestigious new job at the Denver Museum, as I'm sure you know."

"What about the other woman? Did she ever sit for the portrait?"

"Pfft! I don't know, and I don't care. I didn't even know her."

"Do you remember her name?"

"Stacey something, I think. Look, I gotta run. Is there anything else?"

"No, but thank you for your time."

The line went dead.

Tanner sat back in his chair and stared at his notes. He had way more information than he'd expected but nothing solid enough to make an arrest. Still, a noose was beginning to form around Thad Palmer, and Tanner needed to figure out a way to tighten it.

He needed to get with Kate, but she still wasn't in.

He went over to Frank's office.

"Lieutenant?"

"Morning, Tanner. What's up?"

"Have you heard from Kate?"

He shook his head. "Not this morning, but I talked to her Saturday night. She said she had a date on Sunday. Maybe it went well."

Tanner smiled. "We can only hope. That woman needs a social life."

"Well, even so, I'm sure she'll be in any moment."

"I imagine you're right."

Tanner went back to his desk. His mind kept going to a statement made by Palmer in the interview at the museum.

"Detective, it is my personal code to not date nor fraternize with any of my coworkers."

Clearly, that was clearly a lie. So what else was Palmer hiding?

Kate had agreed with him when Tanner suggested the murder of Carole Hampton had not been the first for their killer. If that was true, then there must be cases in Palmer's past. Tanner sat down and searched for the number of the Fort Worth Police Department.

Fort Worth Police Department
Homicide Division
Fort Worth, Texas
10:45 a.m.

Depending on how busy the weekend was, Monday mornings could be crazy busy or slow and steady. For Greg Lassiter, this Monday was following the pattern of slow and steady, which was fine with him. As he neared retirement, his caseload had been reduced, and his focus was on helping clean up some older cases.

Thumbing through a twenty-year-old murder case, he was lost in its details when his phone rang. It took him a minute to grab the receiver, but eventually, he picked up.

"Homicide. Detective Lassiter."

"Good morning. I'm Detective Austin from Denver PD, and I was hoping to speak to someone about your old cases."

Greg laughed. "Well, there's no one older here than me. Will I do?"

"That sounds like as good a qualification as any."

"What can I do for you?"

"I'm working a case up here that involves two females, and my suspect last lived in your city. I was wondering if you had any unsolved cases that matched."

Greg's curiosity was immediately aroused.

"Be glad to help if I can. What have you got?"

"Well, let me start with a name. Thad Palmer."

Greg rolled it around in his brain, but it didn't jar any memories loose.

"Doesn't ring a bell."

"Really? Okay, let's try a description of the M.O." The voice on the other end of the line sounded young, and now, disappointed.

"Let me get a pad and pen; hold on." Greg opened a drawer and retrieved the necessary items. "Okay, shoot."

"I've got two victims. The first is an African-American female, forty-six years-old, found in her bedroom, naked from the waist up. She died from two gunshots fired through a pillow into her forehead. No sign of sexual assault."

Greg scribbled notes, but a case was already coming to mind. "And Vic two?"

"Hispanic female, age twenty-two, also naked from the waist up. She also died from two gunshots to the forehead, again through a pillow, and again with no sign of sexual assault."

Greg's adrenaline was pumping now. "Anything peculiar about the scene?"

"Peculiar?"

"Staging, that sort of thing."

242

"Actually, yes. In both scenes, a piece of furniture was arranged to face the victim. A makeup bench at scene one, and a chair at the second location."

"I may have something for you. Let me pull the file, and I'll call you back. What's your number?"

After writing down the detective's contact information, Greg hung up and went in search of the case they referred to as "Pillow Killings".

Denver Police Department
District 2 Precinct
Holly Street
11:25 a.m.

Tanner waited impatiently for the Fort Worth detective to call back.

He began pacing with his head down, and each time a phone rang and someone beat him to it, he'd spin around to see who'd answered it. If they didn't look up for him, he resumed his pacing.

Each back and forth took him past Kate's desk, which was still empty, a fact that was beginning to eat at him. He'd called her cellphone but got her voicemail. She still had not returned the call.

It had occurred to him she might have gone on a date with Thad Palmer, which made him very uncomfortable in light of what he'd learned, but the possibility seemed so unlikely. Nevertheless, he sat down and called the DAM.

"Denver Art Museum. How can I help you?"

"Thad Palmer, please."

"One minute while I connect you."

He watched the elevator while waiting, hoping to hang up when his partner appeared.

"Modern Art Department."

"Yes, Thad Palmer, please."

"I'm sorry, sir. Mr. Palmer is out of the office today. Can I ask who's calling?"

"Detective Austin with the Denver PD. Was he expected to be out today?"

"No, sir. He called this morning and said he had some personal business to attend to."

The hair on Tanner's neck stood up. *It can't be.*

"Thank you for your help."

He hung up, but before he could make another call to Kate, his phone rang.

"Detective Austin."

"Yeah, it's Greg Lassiter from Fort Worth."

"Hey, Greg. Find anything?"

"I did. We had two murders that matched your description. We referred to them as the Pillow Killing cases. Our scenes are nearly identical to yours. What weapon was used?"

"A .25 caliber."

"That matches. We need to compare slugs."

"Indeed. What about the name Thad Palmer?"

Greg sighed. "He wasn't a suspect in our cases, but after some digging, I did find where he was interviewed by a detective. Apparently, nothing set off any alarms."

"What about dates and the victims' names?"

"Our first case was nearly two years ago. A black female, thirty-eight-year-old Lilly Munson. The second was a white female, twenty-six-year-old Stacey Quick."

The name *Stacey* hit Tanner like a gunshot. "How long ago?"

"Eighteen months."

"Greg, I think I just tied my guy to your second victim."

"You're joking! How?"

"Call this number, and talk with Elaine Prentiss." Tanner read off the number. "She knows of a girl named Stacey who was acquainted with Palmer, and the timeframe matches. Palmer's phone records might make a solid connection."

"Will do. Do you want a copy of my files?"

"Please. Send it as soon as possible. I'll reciprocate as soon as I can, but right now, I need to find Thad Palmer."

Tanner hung up and went to Frank's office. "I've got something, Lieutenant."

"Great! What do you need?"

"A search warrant for the residence of one Thad Palmer."

After handing Frank a piece of paper with the details, Tanner went back to his desk. His cellphone had a message from Kate. Relief swept over him as he called her back.

"This is Kate."

"Where in the name of all that's holy have you been?"

Her tone was instantly apologetic. "I'm so sorry. I'm on my way in now."

"You didn't answer my question."

"I got in late last night and forgot to set my alarm."

Tanner was incredulous, his reaction made worse by the events of the morning. "You overslept!"

"Hey, I am human, you know."

"I know, I know. It's just…you won't believe all that's gone on this morning."

"So, fill me in."

"When you get here, but I have one question about your date yesterday."

"How did you know I had a date?"

"Frank."

"I see. What about it?"

"Was it with Thad Palmer?"

"Definitely not! Why would you ask that?"

"Like I said, I'll fill you in when you get here."

"Okay. I'm twenty minutes out."

Tanner hung up, both relieved and anxious. Relieved that Palmer wasn't with Kate, but anxious over the thought he might be with someone else. And if so, was that someone in danger?

He went to check on that search warrant.

Condominium of Thad Palmer Spire Denver Capitol Hill Neighborhood 1:15 p.m.

Considered, at least by the builder, to be the height of living in the heart of downtown Denver, Spire soared forty-two stories above the city's theater district. It contained nearly five hundred apartments, plus several amenities, such as a spa, a fitness room, an observation deck, and grocery delivery. The place provided the perfect chic headquarters for a man like Thad Palmer.

For that reason, Kate had not been surprised when Tanner had filled her in on what he'd discovered and where the search warrant for Palmer's residence had taken them.

Two patrol cars, each containing a pair of uniformed officers, pulled up behind Tanner and her when they parked on the street outside the tower. They entered the brightly lit lobby and approached a security guard, a young man who appeared to be taken aback by the show of force.

Kate had her badge out. "I'm Detective Walker. We're here to serve a warrant on the apartment of Thad Palmer."

"Okay."

"Do you know if Mr. Palmer is at home?"

"No, but I can call up."

Kate shook her head. "Don't do that. Do you have master keys to the units?"

"The security office does for cases of emergency."

"Mr. Palmer lives in unit 3307, is that correct?"

The guard glanced at his records. "That's right."

"When we exit the elevator, which way do we turn?"

"If you take those elevators over there, you'll turn left when you get off."

Kate was already moving toward the bank of elevators indicated by the young guard.

Tanner glanced at the man. "Please, have someone meet us with the key."

The two detectives and four officers piled into an elevator and rode up to the thirty-third floor. Following the guard's instructions, they exited the elevator and turned left.

"There," Kate said, pointing out unit 3307 about halfway down the hall.

Two officers staged themselves on one side, and two took up positions on the other side of the door. Tanner was holding the warrant, and Kate still had her badge in her hands. She looked at her crew, nodded, then banged on the door.

She waited for a full minute then banged again.

When no response was forthcoming, she pounded harder still.

"Thad Palmer! This is Denver Police. Open up!"

As they waited again, the elevator let off a ding, and the door slid open. The detectives turned to see if it was Palmer. Instead, a man in his mid-fifties, sporting a blue suit and a tie with the Spire logo on it, came toward them.

Tanner stepped over to meet him. "Are you from the security office?"

"Yes, I'm the head of security here. Lorne Hudson."

"You brought a key to the unit?"

"I did."

"Please, let us in."

"I'll need to see your warrant first."

Tanner handed it to him. Hudson looked at it quickly, and apparently having seen one before, handed it back to Tanner. Moving to the entrance, he unlocked the apartment then stepped back.

Kate was first through the open door. "Thad Palmer! This is Denver PD. We have a warrant to search the premises."

The apartment answered with silence.

After the rooms had all been checked, Kate released one set of officers to leave but kept the other pair to watch the doors. Then she and Tanner started meticulously searching the residence.

Tanner started in the kitchen, while Kate moved around the living room.

Wood floors, metal and leather furniture, and large windows gave the place an ultra-modern feel. Kate also noticed the cleanliness of the bachelor pad. If they were right about Palmer, he wasn't just a killer but a fastidious one. That was borne out by the lack of forensic evidence.

Tanner came out of the kitchen. "Nothing in there."

He stopped by the balcony door. "Some view. You can see the Bronco's stadium from here."

Kate rolled her eyes. "You can take a tour and ask about leasing later. How about you search the bedroom next?"

He laughed. "Don't even say that! Laura would love to live here, but I can't afford it on a detective's salary."

She smiled. "Believe me, I know."

Tanner disappeared into the bedroom, while Kate moved over to a small desk near the windows and rifled through the papers on top. Opening the drawers one at time, she found a small appointment book in the second one down.

Several notations were made in dates over the past few weeks. In each case, it had a set of letters and a time. While the times varied, the letters—which appeared to Kate to be initials— were all the same. *JS.*

She laid the book down and continued to open drawers. When she slid the bottom one out, she found herself staring at a box of ammunition. The caliber on the box stood out. *Winchester .25/ACP.*

She looked some more but didn't find the gun.

"Kate!"

"What's up?"

"You better come see this."

She left the ammunition where it was and crossed the apartment to the bedroom door.

"What is it?"

He pointed at the wall over the bed. "Those."

Kate followed his gesture, and her gaze fell on a set of portraits, each done on white paper with a black medium and framed with a simple black frame. They were hung in a row on the wall, and two faces were immediately recognizable. The hair on the back of her neck stood up.

"Is that who I think it is?"

Tanner nodded, stepping close enough to point at the bottom corner of the third one across and read the word someone— presumably the artist—had printed there. "Carole."

He pointed at the fourth portrait.

"Mariel."

"Son of a…"

Tanner nodded toward the other two. "The two cases I told you about in Fort Worth?"

"Yeah."

"Lilly and Stacey. That's them."

Kate moved around to the bottom of the bed, where she could get a better look. It may have been her mind playing tricks on her, but somehow, Palmer seemed to catch overt terror in the eyes of two of his subjects.

"Is it just me, or do you see the fear in Lilly's and Mariel's eyes?"

Tanner shook his head. "It's not you. I see it, too."

"But why those two, only?"

He shrugged. "I know Stacey had some sort of relationship with Palmer, so it's possible Carole did, too. We know she was having an affair with Blackwell; maybe she was seeing Palmer, as well."

"So, what, they were comfortable posing?"

"Who knows? Maybe we see fear in Lilly and Mariel because they were forced into posing."

Kate considered the theory and decided it made as much sense as anything else, which wasn't saying much at that moment.

"We need to bag those."

"Yeah, and then we need to find Palmer."

Kate turned and headed back to the living room. "I might have something on that. Take a look at this."

Tanner followed her to the desk, where Kate showed him the appointment book.

"There are several notations referring to a *JS*. Any idea who that could be?"

Tanner pulled out his notebook and began flipping through the pages. On the fourth or fifth page, he froze.

Kate stared at him. "What?"

Tanner looked up slowly, his eyes widening.

"JS. Joanna Seabrooke."

Kate grabbed her phone and dialed.

"Denver Museum of Art. How can I help you?"

"Joanna Seabrooke, please."

"One moment."

Seconds felt like hours.

"This is Paul Ridley. Can I help you?"

"Mr. Ridley, this is Detective Walker."

"Hi, Detective. What can I do for you?"

"Is Joanna Seabrooke there?"

"Actually, no."

Kate's heart, already beating loud in her ears, now went into overdrive.

"Do you know where she is?"

"She called in and took a personal day is what I was told."

"Do you have her phone number and address?"

"Sure, why?"

"I can't say. Please get them for me."

"Hold on."

The line went to playing some sort of orchestra music, and after nearly five minutes of annoying violins, Ridley returned. He gave her the number and address, and Kate hung up before the educator could ask any more questions.

She dialed Joanna's number. It rang only twice before going to voicemail.

"You've reached Joanna's phone. I'm sorry I'm unavailable, but leave a message, and I promise to call you back."

"Joanna, this is Detective Walker. Please, call me as soon as you get this."

Kate left her number and hung up.

Meanwhile, Tanner had checked the address and punched it into *Google Maps.* "Her place is probably six minutes from here with lights and sirens."

Kate headed for the doorway, pausing long enough to instruct the officers to lock down the apartment, then she ran to the elevator. Tanner was right behind her.

Home of Joanna Seabrooke Block 32 at RiNo Apartments North Denver 3:00 p.m.

"I really appreciate you doing this, Joanna."

She smiled. "You're welcome."

"I've drawn very few people. It requires a lot of commitment to art by the subject, and it takes a lot of emotion out of me to put it on paper."

"I'm touched, Thad. I've never had someone draw me before, and especially not someone who takes it so seriously."

He smiled back at her. "You're very special. By the way, you haven't revealed our relationship to anyone, right?"

"Of course not. We both know what would happen if we're found out."

He nodded and went about getting set up.

Joanna watched as he pulled out a dining chair and positioned it about five feet in front of her. He set his art bag on the floor, leaning against the leg of the chair, and extracted a pad from it. Sitting down to face her, he flipped open the pad, then pulled a black crayon from the bag.

She found his choice of medium interesting. "I can't believe you use a Conté. I make such a mess whenever I try them."

"I've used them for a while now. They seem to capture more emotion, in my opinion."

She was sitting in a recliner, the leg-support kicked up, staring directly at him. Just one light was on, over to her left. He looked up, smiled, and nodded.

"I think we're ready."

"Okay, Sir Rembrandt, draw away."

His smile disappeared. "You need to remove your top and bra."

Her face flushed. "I told you I wasn't doing that!"

"But you know that is a condition of me doing the portrait. It's what I want to capture."

"I thought I made myself clear, but apparently not."

He reached into his art bag and produced a pistol.

Her blood ran cold, and she started to get up, but he vaulted from his chair and cut her off.

He rested the gun against her cheek, and his voice dropped to a hiss. "Take your shirt off, and sit back down—now!"

She obeyed, slowly undoing the buttons down the front of her blouse, while tears welled up in her eyes. "I don't understand, Thad."

"You will. My art is art of significance. It captures a moment in time that only happens once."

Her blouse dropped to the floor. "What moment?"

He ignored her question. "Now the bra!"

When it hit floor, he pointed at the chair with the gun. "Now, back where you were, and resume the pose."

She lowered herself into the recliner, the leather chilling her skin, matching the chill inside her.

He backed away and took his seat again. The gun went into his lap, and he began to draw.

Joanna pushed herself to come up with a plan.

She could bolt for the door but probably wouldn't make it three feet before he gunned her down. She decided she needed to stall, but nothing came to mind. *Think, Joanna. Think.*

She turned and looked toward the bathroom, trying to judge the distance.

"Don't move!"

She jerked and burst into tears, but that seemed to make things worse. The gun came up to point at her.

"And stop crying!"

She did her best to rein in the emotion, telling herself she needed her wits about her to have a chance. "Okay. I'll try."

He continued the drawing, seemingly lost in the deviant manifestation of his art.

She heard them first—sirens.

Moments later, Thad looked up. His hand froze, poised over the drawing, as he listened.

Joanna dared to hope they were coming for her but knew it was unlikely.

No one knew Thad was here with her, and no one was aware of the danger she was in.

When the sirens died before arriving at her door, her heart sank, but not her resolve.

She had almost convinced herself to make a run for it when a knock came at the door.

Thad jumped to his feet, gun in one hand, and grabbed her arm with the other. He pulled her to the front door, his grip extracting a cry of pain, at which point, he wheeled around and pushed his gun into her naked chest.

"Not a noise!"

She nodded.

He dragged her over, where he could look through the peephole. Cussing under his breath, he revealed what he saw. "Walker and Austin!"

Her heart pounded with renewed hope.

Palmer turned to her and pressed a finger against his lips. "Shhhh! We'll wait for them to leave."

The detectives knocked again. Then a third time.

Finally, Detective Walker's voice carried through the door. "Get the building manager. We need to get inside."

Thad's eyes widened. "Crap."

He leaned over and whispered into her ear. "Tell them to wait just a minute."

She nodded. "Just a minute!"

Walker called off the search of the manager. "Hey, forget it."

Palmer, still clutching Joanna's wrist, dragged her back to the living room. "Okay, this is what's gonna happen. You put your top back on, we go to the door, and you get rid of them."

"Okay."

"I'll be right behind the door, and if you screw this up, you and both those detectives are dead. Are we clear?"

"Yes."

"Okay. Get your shirt on."

****

Tanner had come back and joined Kate by the front door of Joanna's apartment.

"You hear something?"

"Yeah. She said just a minute."

The building they were standing in front of was a Scandinavian lookalike, which reminded Tanner of a piece of Ikea, ready-to-assemble furniture. Modern and boring, except for the color, which was bright orange.

Thankfully, Joanna's apartment was a ground-floor unit, giving them more room to maneuver than inside a hallway.

Kate was standing in front of the door, giving a clear view to the peephole, but Tanner took up a position off to the side. A back-up patrol unit had arrived, but Kate had signaled them to wait at their car. Without warning, the lock clicked, and the door cracked open.

"Hi, Detective Walker. Is there a problem?"

"No, not if everything is okay with you."

"I'm fine. Why wouldn't I be?"

Kate stepped a little closer, peering behind Joanna.

"Do you mind if we come in? We'd like to ask you a few questions."

Joanna opened the door a little more, then made an exaggerated eye roll toward the back of the door. "It's not really a good time…"

Fear radiated from the girl's eyes, and her hands trembled.

Kate looked at Tanner. He nodded that he's seen the signal.

Kate's voice never wavered. "I see. Perhaps later then?"

"If you don't mind."

Through the space by the door hinges, Tanner spotted a shape. He looked at Kate, who was watching him out of the corner of her eye. He pointed at her, and nodded toward Joanna. Then tapped his chest and gestured toward the door.

Kate nodded, raising her voice noticeably. "That will work out fine."

Tanner drew his weapon and steeled himself for the moment Kate took action.

She pulled out a business card and extended it to Joanna, careful to keep her hand outside the doorframe. When Joanna reached for the card, Kate grabbed her arm and jerked her forward, the two of them falling onto the cement walkway.

At the same instant, Tanner threw himself against the front door, driving Palmer back against the wall. A gun dropped to the ground, and as Tanner recoiled, Palmer reached for the weapon.

Tanner drove his shoulder into the door again, smashing Palmer against the wall for the second time. Palmer slumped to the floor, temporarily dazed. Tanner kicked the gun down the hall.

Palmer looked up, confusion on his face, his eyes glassy, and blood seeping from his nose.

Tanner shoved the man facedown, pulled one wrist and slapped a cuff on it, then did the same to the other.

"Thad Palmer, you're under arrest for murder. Anything you say, can and will be used against you in a court of law. You have the right..."

One of the back-up officers arrived at the door. Tanner handed his prisoner over with disgust.

"You read him his rights, then get him out of here."

Tanner went outside, where he found Kate and Joanna sitting in the grass. Joanna was shaken but apparently unhurt. Kate was smiling.

"Nice work, Austin."

"Thank you, ma'am."

The uniform officer came by, dragging his prisoner by the cuffs.

After watching Palmer shoved into the patrol car, Tanner grinned down at Kate.

"And to think you and Thad could have been an item!"

She rolled her eyes. "Like I said, he's not my type."

Joanna had recoiled when Palmer walked by but now she was staring toward the patrol car.

"He's nobody's type anymore."

Tanner laughed. "When you're right, you're right!"

An EMT showed up, and checked out both women.

Tanner was leaning against their car, making some notes, when Kate caught up with him. He looked over her shoulder toward the ambulance. "Is she going to be all right?"

"Yeah. She skinned an elbow when we landed on the cement, but that's it."

"You mean besides the emotional trauma."

"Yeah, besides that!"

He finished his notes, and when he looked up, he realized she was watching him.

She sighed. "I guess I'll have to tell Frank I think you're going to work out."

Tanner grinned. "I appreciate that, but I admit I'm still in need of an experienced detective to keep me out of trouble."

Kate's smile was warm. "I'm sure you'll find someone to take you on."

DENVER HOMICIDE

<u>Tuesday, April 14</u>

Denver Police Department
District 2 Precinct
Holly Street
4:45 p.m.

Much of the previous night and the next day were devoted to taking statements, processing evidence, booking Palmer, and the infinite number of details that needed to be taken care of before the case was passed off to the prosecutor's office.

Having done all these things many times, for Kate, much of it had been routine. However, she had made a point to visit the Reynas and tell them of the arrest. The faith Mrs. Reyna had shown in Kate had made her even more determined. It felt good to reward that trust.

She spent part of the morning looking back at the biggest case of her career and comparing it to this one. The sense of accomplishment she had then was equal to what she felt now. The euphoria of pulling Joanna Seabrooke from under the nose of Thad Palmer and of knowing the young woman was safe, was equaled by just one other case—Missy Noland.

Twice now, she'd experienced the ultimate reward for a detective, and she recognized how fortunate she was.

Tanner was at his desk, still filling out reports, when she stood and headed to Frank's office. The lieutenant, much like everyone else at the precinct, was in high spirits.

She tapped on the doorframe. "Got a minute?"

"Of course." He waved her in. "What's up?"

Kate entered and closed the door.

"I wanted to talk to you about Austin."

"Okay. Shoot."

"You were right."

"I know. What about?"

She laughed. "He's smart, and he has tremendous instincts."

"I'm sure he'd find that to be a real compliment coming from you."

"He's still pretty raw, though."

Frank nodded but his expression remained serious. "Indeed. He could use a steady hand to bring him along."

"Yeah, to be sure. I thought I'd hang around and work with him some more."

Frank looked as if he was hurting himself trying to keep a straight face. "He could use someone of your expertise."

"So, I guess you can ignore the transfer request."

"Still need a challenge in your life, huh?"

"Something like that."

Frank was grinning widely now and pulled out the transfer request. "Would you like to do the honors, or should I?"

"You can."

He tore it in half and let the two pieces float into the trashcan. "Done."

"There is one thing, though."

"Which is?"

"Your buddy took you to a Shakespeare festival to make his point. I didn't get a Hendrix concert."

He laughed. "That's right, so there's a lesson to be learned."

"What's that?"

"Next time I tell you a story, pick a living rock star!"

****

Tanner was watching the door to Frank's office with one eye and his report with the other. As a result, he didn't see the woman standing in front of him arrive.

"Is Detective Walker in?"

Tanner looked up to see a blonde young lady in her twenties, smiling brightly.

"Uh...yeah. She's in with the lieutenant."

"Okay. I'm meeting her and my father here. Can I wait somewhere?"

"Sure. Kate's desk is over there. You can sit in front of it."

"Thank you."

"Can I tell her who is here?"

"Missy, Missy Noland."

Tanner just stared at her, which apparently made Missy uncomfortable. "Is there something wrong?"

"No... No, of course not. You said your father was coming, too?"

"Yes. David Noland. Do you know him?"

He shrugged. "I don't know. Should I?"

"He's the comptroller for Denver Light Rail."

Tanner's jaw was hanging open, but he managed to pull it together long enough to say, "I'm sure Kate will be out any minute."

He got up and moved over by the lieutenant's door, planning to ambush his partner when she emerged. After just a few moments, the door swung open, and Kate ran right into him.

"Were you listening through the door?"

Tanner shook his head. "Nope. Just wanted to say your visitor has arrived."

"David?"

"Nope, again. Missy Noland."

Kate's head swiveled. "She's here?"

"Right over there by your desk."

Tanner watched Kate practically run to the young woman, who stood and embraced Kate.

Tanner followed slowly, not wanting to intrude. Kate nodded toward him.

"Missy, this is my partner, Tanner Austin."

Tanner wagged a finger at Kate.

"Soon to be ex-partner, don't you mean?"

Kate shook her head. "No. Partner is what I meant."

For the second time in ten minutes, Tanner was speechless.

Kate poked him in the chest. "Close your mouth, Austin. You're letting in flies."

David Noland walked up. "I see I'm late to the party."

Kate went over and kissed his cheek. "You didn't tell me you were inviting Missy."

"She wouldn't let me."

Kate was beaming. "Well, it's great to see her."

"I told her about our day together on Sunday. When she learned we were having dinner tonight, she wouldn't take no for an answer."

Kate turned to Tanner. "You mind if I bail out a little early?"

He laughed. "Mind? I wish you would. Your social gathering is preventing me from getting any work done."

Kate smiled at him warmly. "See you in the morning, then?"

"Yes, ma'am, but try not to oversleep."

She glared at him quickly. "Careful, Rookie!"

JOHN C. DALGLISH

Get a *FREE copy of the ebook*

"WHERE'S MY SON?"

Detective Jason Strong - #1

Visit this link.
http://jcdalglish.webs.com/

OTHER LINKS:
jdalglish7@gmail.com
https://www.facebook.com/DetectiveJasonStrong

****

Author's Note

As Homicide #5 comes out, I am amazed at how many have written reviews, letters, and shown support for us and for the books. It is a privilege to put these out and have so many say they enjoy them. It's very encouraging when people say they look forward to the next one.

DENVER HOMICIDE

To all of you, thank you from the bottom of our heart. You're helping make our dreams come true.

God Bless, John
I John 1:9

Cover by Beverly Dalglish
Edited by Jill Noelle-Noble
Proofreading by Robert Toohey

****

Other Clean Suspense Books

By

John C. Dalglish

THE CITY MURDERS SERIES

BOSTON HOMICIDE - #1
MIAMI HOMICIDE - #2

274

JOHN C. DALGLISH

CHICAGO HOMICIDE - #3
DALLAS HOMICIDE - #4
DENVER HOMICIDE - #5

THE DETECTIVE JASON STRONG SERIES

"WHERE'S MY SON?" - #1
BLOODSTAIN - #2
FOR MY BROTHER - #3
SILENT JUSTICE - #4
TIED TO MURDER - #5
ONE OF THEIR OWN - #6
DEATH STILL - #7
LETHAL INJECTION - #8
CRUEL DECEPTION - #9
LET'S PLAY - #10
HOSTAGE - #11
CIRCLE OF FEAR - #12
DEADLY OBSESSION - #13
DEAD OF NIGHT - #14
SHADOW OF NIGHT - #15

DENVER HOMICIDE

THE CHASER CHRONICLES